SOLDIER, Princess, REBEL SPY

by

Karen Harris Tully

Blue Zephyr Press
2661 N. Pearl, #360
Tacoma WA 98407

This book is a work of fiction. Names, characters, and incidents are products of the author's imagination or are used fictiously. Any resemblance to actual events or persons living or dead is entirely coincidental.

Cover art by **LILT**.

ISBN-10: 1-7320863-1-1
ISBN-13: 978-1-7320863-1-9

Galactic Dreams

What if somewhere out in the future a heroine must save a girl who is already dead?

What if on a planet with no sky a woman with no wings could fly?

What if on a lonely moon there was a prince who could only be rescued by the girl who came to kill him?

Welcome to the universe of Galactic Dreams, where fairy tales are reimagined for a new age—the future. In each Galactic Dreams novella you'll find an old tale reborn with a mixture of romance, technology, aliens and adventure. But beware, a perilous quest awaits behind every star and getting home again will depend on a good spaceship, true love, and maybe just a hint of magic.

Galactic Dreams is a unique series of science-fiction novellas from Blue Zephyr Press featuring retellings of classic tales from different authors, all sharing the same universe, technology, and history.

We hope you enjoy this adventure.

Table of Contents

SOLDIER, PRINCESS, REBEL SPY

Prologue

COLONY PLANET LYRIC. FIFTEEN YEARS AGO.

An eight-year-old girl crawled into bed in a farmhouse attic, next to a window, under a towering mulberry tree. She turned off her dented vid machine, sighing at one last picture of the handsome, fair-skinned prince, almost the same age she was, relaxing in his far away moon palace.

"Grandmama, tell me a princess story?" she asked with a yawn, as her grandmother tucked the quilt, a colorful patchwork made from scraps of silk, under her chin with hands dyed a muted rainbow of muddled hues. Her family hand-blended only the richest colors for the Empress and her Royal court on their moon—the Jewel of Gallaius.

"Ah, Meilin," Grandmama sighed, but gave her an indulgent smile. "You know we have no princesses, my dear, not here on Lyric, and the Royals are worlds away."

"But you tell such good stories. Please, Grandmama?"

"Oh, all right, but only until your parents come to kiss you goodnight, and then I have more to do."

"You always have more." Meilin pouted.

Her grandmother laughed and got a faraway look in her eyes. "Yes. How about an old story then, about a lonely princess and a handsome stable boy, who together decided to change their stars?"

"Oh yes please, Grandmama! That's my favorite."

"Very well. Lay back and close your eyes. It all began when an ex-princess and her ex-stable boy exchanged rings beneath a mulberry tree."

"Like that one out there?" Meilin sat up and pointed out the window at the old tree on the hill, the oldest on the farm.

"Yes, dear." Grandmama waited until Meilin lay back down. "But before that, a lonely princess, on a gilded Royal moon, climbed the Empress's rose arbor, on a dare from a handsome stable boy…"

Chapter 1:

MEILIN - REBEL STARSHIP HMS TEMERITY, PRESENT DAY

"Wei!" the drill sergeant barked from across the training center of the Rebel cruiser, hidden behind the nearest rocky moon of colony planet, Lyric. All the trainees stopped and looked up from their workouts and wrestling matches, waiting for the officer to complete his order. Meilin too, paused in her sparring match with a new recruit and looked over at the shout of her name. Her opponent however, who was at least four times bigger than she was, did not, and backhanded her hard, right across the cheekbone. She fell to her knees. Damn, that would teach her to not take eyes off the new guy. She wiped blood from her nose.

"Ha! Told you losers I could take her in a fair fight," he crowed to the other trainees. "Look, I hit her so hard, her anti-rec screen is imprinted on my hand." He laughed and held up the back of his hand for the crowd to see the dark and light triangular patches she had painted unevenly across her cheeks that morning. Other swirls, spots, and thick lines obscured her features to the government's surveillance probes, though it should be unnecessary amidst the Rebels. She liked to stay in practice. Her dark straight hair, held a streak of blue hanging over one eye, completing her ever-changing look. No one ever truly knew what Wei Meilin looked like under the makeup, and she wanted to keep it that way.

She shook off the late hit and the room fell silent.

She had indeed promised this new recruit a fair fight, and fair was fair. From her position on her knees, she threw an uppercut, fast and hard into his man bits. He froze for a second before crumpling to the mat.

"Wei Meilin!" Sergeant Xiaobo yelled more insistently.

"Coming!" she yelled back. "Seriously? The *shinse* I have to put up with to kill the Empress," she grumbled, testing her cheek as she made her way through the silent Rebel trainees toward the officer.

But the guy on the mat wheezed after her. "You *biao-zi.*"

She stopped with a sigh, then whipped around and flicked her hand, her middle finger arcing a white-hot bolt of energy at him.

"There," she said to those surrounding the twitching new guy. "When he wakes up you can tell him he won." She endured a withering glare from Sergeant Xiaobo before he turned and led the way to the Commander's office. Well, no big loss there; Xiaobo had never liked her anyway. She waited outside while the Sergeant filled in the Commander.

"Wei Meilin, get in here!" Commander Zhang barked.

Meilin stepped inside and saluted her unforgiving CO. She'd been training tirelessly for six years now. She had been a scared, angry seventeen-year-old when she'd arrived. She was no longer scared, but she was still angry. She had learned to fight and to control her unique plague "Gift"—well most of the time—and she hoped she was finally about to get her long-awaited assignment. It was her dream to infiltrate the Royal guard in the moon palace, the Jewel of Gallaius, and oust corrupt Empress Ming-Zhu. She'd gladly give up her Gift to have her family back, but since that wasn't possible, she was more than ready to avenge their deaths.

"Meilin, you know we can't have you electrocuting the other trainees." The Commander seemed tired of reminding her.

"He'll be fine, Commander. Besides, you used to say I needed all the practice I could get."

The Commander pursed her lips and said wryly. "You've been all practiced up for a while now. And your time has finally come. The Rebellion is ready for the next step in our plan." The CO turned around to retrieve a com pad from the desk behind her.

Yes! Meilin pumped her fists silently and did a little jig in place. She froze again as the Commander turned back toward her, looking down at the com pad.

"You'll be infiltrating the palace—"

Yes! Yes, Yes, Yes! She was sooo ready to kick some Royal a—

"—as a princess candidate."

Her previously dancing insides froze. "A *what?*"

"A princess candidate. There is a call out for girls age eighteen to twenty-four with Royal bloodlines. It seems our dear Prince is looking for a bride."

"A bride! But Ma'am, I'm a soldier, not a princess. And besides, I don't have Royal blood," she felt a triumphant surge of relief, but it was short lived.

"Ah, but your new documents *say* that you do." The Commander pushed a file folder across the desk toward her. "A blood test showing two point four percent royalty from your great, great, grandfather. Who knew?" She shrugged sarcastically at the results of the fake blood test. "I know you've trained as a soldier, but this is too good a chance to pass up."

"But," Meilin was horrified, "I can't marry the Prince!" She remembered that pale, lazy, pretty boy from the vid feeds years ago when she'd still lived on her family's farm, and had still believed in fairy tales.

"And we don't need you to. I don't care if you say two words to him. Your assignment is to fit in enough to be able to move around the palace undetected. Your job will be to use your Gift to pre-charge and ready the EMP, the Electro-Mag Pulse bomb we are sneaking in prior to our invasion. You will be tasked with significant changes to its guidance system, as it will arrive on the Royal moon disguised as a present; fireworks from a generous loyal to celebrate the Prince's engagement. The Royals will launch the fireworks rocket the night of the Prince's engagement ball, when he announces his choice for princess. Our forces will arrive to stage our coup during the ensuing chaos. This is imperative, Meilin. Our coup is resting on your shoulders. So I need to know, can you pull this off?"

Meilin took a deep breath and straightened her shoulders. As long as she could get close to the Empress, she didn't care how. She'd prance through the palace buck naked if that's what it took.

"Count on me, Ma'am."

"Good. You'll go with Yun now." As if from nowhere, a lithe young woman with iridescent purple hair and bejeweled rainbow eyebrows appeared at her elbow with a nod to Meilin. "You need to look the part of a princess and she's in charge of making sure you do and providing support during your mission. Go. You don't have much time before your transport leaves tomorrow."

Meilin allowed the young woman to lead her, passing an older man on their way out the door. He was a big man, tall and rotund with ruddy skin, dressed in a politician's slick smile and a formal court suit. Meilin recognized him immediately as Governor Fong, the Crown appointed leader of Lyric. He held a fancy box that was already open with the top tucked under, revealing a pale blue, glowing fruit resting on padded folds of red velvet. She stared. What was *he* doing on the Rebel ship, bringing presents to Commander Zhang?

"My dear Commander!" he exclaimed, striding into her office. She accepted the box while making shooing motions at Meilin and Yun with one hand. The door shut as soon as they were over the threshold.

Count on me, Ma'am. Twelve hours later, she was fully regretting those words. She'd been plucked, lasered, and sand-blasted, wrapped, squeezed, and shaped, puttied, masked, stripped, and lacquered to within an inch of her sanity. Almost every bit of skin was hairless and polished to a high gloss shine. The only hair she'd been allowed to keep were her eyebrows and eyelashes, as she was told they were a mark of status where she was going, the Royal moon, the Jewel of Gallaius.

Under the domes of the Jewel, every bit of breathable air and drinkable water had to be manufactured, purified, and recirculated over and over, and so, cleanliness was the height of fashion. Every person on the Jewel scrubbed every bit of their skin daily, before it, and any hairs, could slough off and become dust to clog the filters, or worse, part of the air they all breathed. The only people allowed to grow real hair were the Empress and her son the Prince. Instead, small holograph emitters were worn atop the bare heads of the court, allowing them to wear the illusion of any hairstyle they wished, providing it didn't outshine the Empress.

Currently, Meilin was staring at herself in a mirror, without makeup for the first time in years. Her shiny scalp was striking, but what she really noticed was her resemblance to her beloved Grandmama, lost thankfully years before the plague ravaged her town and killed her parents. She was glad her grandparents had not lived to see their family unable to pay their full tithe to the Crown, and the Royals' response of withholding the cure.

She forced herself not to get lost in the past and instead looked at the rest of her reflection. She was wearing the most restrictive, constrictive dress in a horrid periwinkle color, and matching, ridiculous platform shoes that clunked hollowly as she walked. And her nails were painted. Pink. She tapped them on the control plate to change them to a deep blue with tiny sparkles that resembled the starry night sky, and then again, changing them to the exact golden yellow of the mulberry candies her family used to make for the palace. She left the color as a reminder.

She tottered up the transport ramp and collapsed onto a padded seat bench of the non-descript shuttle she'd be taking to Lyric and the princess candidate transport, and then on to the Royal moon. She stood back up and sneered at her reflection in the shuttle window. She looked like a Loyal. Only those with nothing to hide from the Crown's drones went around bare-faced. She straightened and practiced the stupid smile she thought a princess would wear. This was her assignment and she was determined to succeed.

But first, she had to learn to walk in these god-forsaken shoes.

Chapter 2:

MEILIN - MEETING THE EMPRESS

The Empress was looking thin, Meilin thought, keeping her pleasant smile in place, like a mask over her feelings at seeing her parents' murderer in the flesh. She did not mean it as a compliment, either. The latest vid feeds she had seen of the Empress before leaving Lyric were out of date, she knew, but she hadn't expected the chubby, smiling matriarch to have changed into the cold, thin woman who sat before them now on her golden throne. She was talking quietly with one of her advisors, who was shaking his shiny, bald head. She banged her fist against the arm of her throne unhappily.

Meilin felt the lumpy, silken bag of the Empress's favorite candies in the cleverly hidden pocket of her donated gown. Patience, she had to wait for just the right time, a time when the Empress's Royal tasters were not around.

She looked at the girls in line to her left and right. There were fifteen of them total, awaiting their audience with the Empress, having just arrived from Lyric after being stuck on a transport together for the last two days. Meilin didn't know how, but each of them still somehow managed to look more serene and lovely than the last. But Meilin wasn't sizing up her competition for Prince Cormorin's hand. She schooled her features into the genteel smile she'd practiced a hundred times since receiving her assignment. She fingered her forged Royal papers in her skirt pocket.

The Jewel of Gallaius, the moon palace of their destroyed

home world, had shone brightly from space when they'd arrived, a beautiful group of luminescent soap bubbles on the surface of the rocky moon. Each girl had had a change in status as soon as the request came through from their Empress. The girls from Lyric with any Royal lineage were suddenly princess material, and needed at Royal court. Apparently, there were no suitable young women on the moon from which Prince Cormorin could choose his bride.

Meilin barely managed to keep her disgusted snort to herself as they waited for the Empress, seated on her giant, golden throne, to finish her hushed conversation. Meilin was no princess, and she had no intention of competing for the hand of a ridiculous, pompous prince.

Being inside the Great Room of the moon palace, part ballroom, part throne room, felt like being inside a gilded egg. The gold leaf trim on the walls was of course from Lyric, as was the glass for the domed ceiling and one entire wall made up of floor to ceiling windows. The rainbow chandelier that sent multicolored light bouncing around the ostentatious room must have also been imported from Lyric. The rocky moon had nothing to mine but iron ore, pumice and gypsum, and the sandy moon soil produced only dusky black glass, not the sparkling jewel tones above that threw rainbows around the Great Room like confetti.

The silk drapes covering the floor-to-ceiling windows, blocked the view of planet Gallaius. That and the fine silk covering the chairs, those materials were more personal to Meilin, coming not just from Lyric, but in the past, they would have come from her own family's farm. But it had been six years since the farm had burned to the ground. They must have found another producer by now.

As the Empress continued talking with a thin, pompous man, rather than addressing her summoned audience, Meilin surveyed her enemy. The Empress was regal of course. She wore her real hair long and black, towering above her head in thin braids that waved like live serpents, charmed to dance atop her head with an anti-grav device. Empress Ming-Zhu was a formidable sight in her green, patterned silk. However, it ruined the effect each time she absently adjusted and itched under the high collar. Meilin couldn't hold back her smirk this time. Her family's silk would never have caused such discomfort.

She schooled her features again into serenity as the Princesses around her twittered up and down the line. The Prince had just walked in, and she caught her breath. He was, she had to admit, better looking now than the spoiled prince she'd seen on the old vids. He'd filled out nicely in the intervening years, no doubt thanks to an extensive gym somewhere in the palace. And he sported a glowing tan, which must have come from some device considering the sun was heavily filtered by the moon's domes. He wore an ornate military uniform and shiny boots, though she doubted the sword attached to his belt was more than decorative.

That's where she should be, the Royal military. It was what she'd trained for, to work her way into the Royal guard. Instead, Meilin had landed here, with only a few day's preparation before being handed her fake royalty papers, stuffed into this ill-fitting dress, and herded onto the Royal transport.

He strode quickly over to the throne next to his mother's and sat, leaning insolently over one arm of his throne to say something impatiently to his mother. She waved her hand at him to wait and he turned to survey the girls lined up for his perusal like the catch of the day. His eyes assessed Meilin for a long moment before moving on. She kept her meaningless smile in place and only after he'd moved on did she realize that she ought to have curtsied or something, like the other girls. She sighed, hoping she wouldn't give herself away this early.

I am a princess, I am a princess. I am a damn prissy, prissy princess, she chanted silently. Success required that she pull this off. After he'd looked over the rest of his choices, his Royal insufferableness came back to her. This time she dropped into a practiced curtsy, teeth gritted in a smile the whole time, in deference to his accident of birth. He looked briefly disappointed. Whatever. She had no need to impress him, she only had to fit in enough to gain access to the palace and set the Rebellion's plans in motion.

Her contacts in the Rebellion had trumped up some long ago, vague relationship to royalty for her, but that must be all that half of these girls had, except of course for Celestine Fong, whose father was the governor of Lyric and who could trace her lineage back to Lord and Lady Fong, exiled to the new world only four generations ago. But Meilin guessed that their exile hardly mattered now. Celestine's paperwork, as she'd shown off at every opportunity on the trip to the palace, showed that she was 12.5% Royal, which she held up as proof that she was destined to be the next Empress herself, rather than a tool to bring new blood to the fading Royal line and strengthen ties to their colony, Lyric.

The girl, Celestine, was as blonde as Meilin was dark, and

everything else that Meilin was not. Tall, statuesque and curvy, beautiful and grandiose, and she knew all the court etiquette like she'd been born to it. Her best friend and rival, Kaletra Kineret, was also a shoe-in for the princess-ship, if haughty bombast was a good measure. Though apparently, she only scored 9.8% on the royalty test.

Out of fifteen girls, Meilin had only made one friend on the trip to court, Imogen, who had quickly confided that she felt as out of place amongst royalty as Meilin did. They'd quickly bonded with their shared farm-girl upbringings, though Meilin had avoided giving too many details of her life before the princess contest.

As for Meilin, her papers showed a paltry 2.4%, hardly Royal at all, but enough to get her on the ship to the Royals' moon. From her spot in line, she tried to catch a glimpse of planet Gallaius, nearly destroyed some seventy-five years ago in an idiotic nuclear war that radiated the planet and killed everyone on it. The Royals had been the only ones to receive enough warning and with the option of escape to their military moon base. But the floor to ceiling silk brocade curtains seemed strategically closed to offer only views of space.

The Empress was still talking with her advisor and the handsome Prince was now frowning with a finger to one ear and looking at something on a com on his wrist. Sports no doubt. Meilin stepped out of line and walked the short distance over to the nearest window and pulled aside the heavy drape.

"Pssst! What are you doing? Get back here!" she heard from one of the girls behind her. She looked back to see a girl named Orencia waving frantically at her to come back. The Royals were still ignoring them. Meilin waved at Orencia and a few other girls that looked aghast at her nerve.

"Come look," she mouthed at them. A few looked tempted, but they all stayed in their places. Meilin shrugged and pulled the curtain aside to see the destroyed planet of her grandparents' birth. She caught her breath and stepped fully behind the curtain, putting her hands on the cold glass, the breath she released immediately creating a fog. She moved a step over and held her breath.

It was huge and surprisingly beautiful. She'd expected a brown, cratered rock, but gorgeous blues and vivid greens took up most of the field of view. She wondered if this was what those first, brave colonists had seen centuries ago as they came out of hyper-sleep from their long journey from Earth.

She glanced to either side out the window and saw to one side a gleaming silver ring in the distance, the long inert jump gate built by those first colonists to speed transport to and from Earth. Over time, they'd realized that having a jump gate so close to a populated planet was asking for some sort of world-ending accident, hence a two day journey to Lyric. And on the other side, she saw the surface of the unimpressive, dark rock of the moon she stood on, where those first Terran colonists had placed their military base. She bet they never thought their great, great, many times great grandchildren would have their palace here, and would be squeezing another far-off colony dry in their thirst for tithe money and goods.

A commotion behind her pulled her out of her reverie. "You there! What do you think you're doing?" a Royal voice snapped and a hairless servant pulled her unceremoniously back to the lineup of wannabe princesses. The Empress glared at her, awaiting her response. The Prince merely looked intrigued.

Meilin curtsied to the Empress, but kept her head high. "I was looking at Gallaius, Your Majesty. It is really quite beautiful."

"It is *not* beautiful, insolent girl. It is destroyed! I have half a mind to put you right back on that transport to that pond scum planet you came from."

And Meilin had half a mind to throw the bag of golden candies in her pocket at the Empress's murdering head, but she reminded herself that she was made of stronger stuff. She dropped another damn curtsey.

"My Empress," she murmured demurely.

The Empress grunted and waved a hand. "Proceed." Meilin wondered if she was going to be booted after all and fail her mission before it had even begun when two medics, hairless as were all staff members, started going down the line of girls with a glowing white device that they pressed into each girl's wrist in turn. The gun came away beeping a countdown, leaving a drop of blood on the girls' wrists which another tech quickly bandaged, and the first medic read a number from the hand-held screen.

"Eight point four percent Royal blood," he read officially for the first girl. Oh good gods what was this now? "Six point three percent," he read for the second and, "Ten point nine," for the third. The girls shifted in line so that the girl with the highest number was first in line to meet the Empress and Prince. Celestine soon held that position with her rating of "twelve point six percent Royal blood."

Meilin began to sweat. She was about to be found out before

she'd had any chance of completing her mission.

"We've received word that one of you may be an imposter sent by Rebels," the Empress soothed as some of the girls started to twitter. "It is merely a small blood test to ensure each of you belong here." The girls already tested looked at the rest of the girls in line as if wondering which one was the imposter.

Shinse. And she'd be thrown in the Royal dungeon as a spy. Meilin grasped the folded papers in her pocket and started taking short shallow breaths, locking her knees for good measure. She was going to have to act her ass off.

The medic finally pronounced the girl in front of Meilin, "Four point two percent Royal blood," in his nasal voice and turned to her. Instead of holding out her wrist, she held one arm to her forehead and fanned her face with her papers in her other hand. She stepped away from the medic and addressed the Empress.

"Your Majesty, I am so embarrassed. Giving blood makes me terribly queasy. I fear I must, I must..." It had been several minutes of short quick breaths now and they were doing their job. She didn't have to fake the sweat on her face or her racing heart. She closed her eyes and fanned herself more vigorously, taking one deep breath. Her hands were starting to tingle and she didn't want to overdo it if she had to run. "Of course, I brought my family papers with me." She offered them to the head medic, whose superiority was obvious because he'd been allowed to keep his eyebrows.

But the Empress was glaring at Meilin. "Hold her," she snapped and before Meilin could move, two guards appeared at her sides and grabbed her arms. She took another deep breath, she was going to need it now, and prepared to fight, but the medic was quick as a wraith. She felt the small prick on her wrist before she could whip the guards' arms backward and break away.

They released her and she stared at the small drop of blood on her wrist in real horror.

She was so screwed.

Her mind raced. Did she fight her way through the guards blocking the door? Did she let this play out? She really hadn't trained for this.

She put her hand over her mouth as if sick and ran for the door, trying to push her way through the guards and counting the medic device's beeps. It would only chirp five times before the results were announced. Any moment she was sure she would hear that nasally voice sneer, "Zero point zero percent Royal."

And she'd be arrested.

And this guard was not getting out of her way.

And she really did think that she was going to puke now.

Instead she jabbed her fist out, right into the guard's throat, and spun for the next one. Just then she heard, "Twenty-eight point one two five percent Royal." The medic's voice held absolute shock.

The whole room stopped, except for that guard falling and choking on the pristine marble floor. And Meilin ran through the door.

Chapter 3:

She fled to the bathroom and locked the door, sure that any moment they'd rerun the test, and proclaim it all a big mistake. Or a joke. She looked at her glistening face in the gilded mirror above the wash basin. She really was going to hyperventilate and pass out now.

Twenty-eight point whatever percent? How was that even possible? Unless…. She traced cheekbones and dark eyebrows in the mirror that were so reminiscent of her late Grandmama's.

And the Princess and the stable boy fled by shuttle, into the everlasting night of space, headed for the colony planet, Lyric….

"Princess?" She heard the medic's voice outside the door, now tinged with awe and deference. "Your… Highness? Are you all right in there?"

"I-" She spun for the toilet. She didn't even have to put her fingers down her throat to make herself puke.

After a minute, she shakily decided she was done and stood up. Going back to the sink, she splashed water on her admittedly pale face. Her dark brown eyes stared back in shock from her thin face—she wasn't used to seeing herself without her anti-rec screen. Yun had insisted she outline her almond eyes to go with her new holo-hair, which was straight and black to her waist, like her real hair had been, before the plague. Yun had called her choice of black boring. She could wear shimmering peacock feathers, or a rainbow sunset on her head, but Meilin preferred the nostalgia of what had once been.

Now she took a deep breath and tried to get her face to settle into something that didn't scream that she'd just received the shock of her life.

She opened the door to the hall to find it, not filled with people as she'd expected, but with only one person present. Prince Cormorin leaned arrogantly against the wall. What right did anyone from his family have to look *that* good? He had a strong jaw and perfectly straight nose, and deep brown eyes that were the exact color of really good, dark cocobenne. He had short, real, dark hair that was tousled like he'd just run his hands through it, and he was tan, in the way that no one on the Jewel was tan, due to the heavy solar filtration of the domes. She wondered if his stylist had suggested he visit a tanning pod to follow Lyran fashion, or if it was his idea. He smacked something against his leg, and she saw her forged papers that she'd dropped in her haste. He pinned her with a look.

"You knuckle punched my guard in the throat," he said.

"Well, I was about to puke in front of the Empress," Meilin replied, dropping into a curtsy a beat too late.

"No need for that." He jerked his hand at her to rise before continuing. "He was down, unable to breathe for at least two minutes."

"He was blocking my way."

"You've obviously trained in fighting, and yet, you throw up at the sight of a drop of blood?"

"Only mine," she snapped. "Phobias aren't always rational, Your Highness."

"Yeah, about that." He lifted her forged family lineage papers. "Says here you barely have any Royal blood. Two point four percent. What happened there?"

"They just went by our family records on file with the Governor. They needed one more girl to fill Her Majesty's quota and here I am."

"You mean to say that you didn't *know* that your grandma was the lost princess?" he asked incredulously.

She stared at him. Had Grandmama really been lost?

"Apparently, Grandmama had a secret. I guess not everyone wants to be Royal."

He gave her a look like she was one black hole short of a quasar. "Apparently not." He turned away shaking his head.

"Oh, pardon me!" Meilin dropped into a low curtsy to his back. "Was this where the ass-kissing was supposed to begin, Highness?"

He tossed a glare over his shoulder and kept walking.

"I'm just here for the food!" she called after him, then leaned back against the wall, alone in the hallway. She probably shouldn't have done that. That blood test had granted her some weird sort of reprieve. Her mission wasn't screwed after all. But she could forget blending in with the other girls now, and antagonizing the Prince wouldn't help. It was just that something about his muscle-y privilege provoked her.

And now, what was a newly minted Princess supposed to do? She wished she could just disappear to her room and hide, but they hadn't been shown to their rooms yet. She could either go back to the Great Room so everyone could stare at her, or she could explore the palace. She set off in the direction opposite the Great Room.

Chapter 4:

CORMORIN · PRIORITIES

"Here for the food, indeed," Cor muttered to himself, heading back to the Great Room. So much for his mother telling him for weeks that any of these girls would be thrilled at the prospect of marrying him. Apparently, she was wrong about at least one of them. While he hadn't wanted to be pushed into getting married, he had to admit that being surrounded by good looking young women competing for his time and attention hadn't sounded so bad. Now he wasn't so sure.

Since his mother hadn't listened to his wishes over her yes-addicted advisors, he'd planned to go along with this ridiculous contest until it came time to declare his bride. And then, he'd make his point to his mother, the Empress. He would find a girl and settle down when he was good and ready, and not before. It wasn't like she was going to banish her only son.

However, she had been acting strangely lately, seeming hazy and following nearly anything an advisor suggested at times, as if it were her own idea. But at other times, she was ill-tempered, unwilling to listen to reason. And this contest was an unfortunate result. Her Royal physician had said she was well, in excellent health, but Cor still had his doubts.

Right now, he only hoped the other girls weren't as insufferable as that pale, black haired one. He checked the papers still in his hand for her name, Wei Meilin, and grunted. She was small and slender, looking like the solar wind might blow her straight off the Jewel's surface, given the chance. But when she'd needed to escape the Great Room in a hurry for the bathroom, visibly and audibly ill, she'd chosen the weakest link in his guard and dropped him with one well-placed punch. That was more than instinctive self-preservation, and he wondered what she would have done next to get out. He'd have to keep an eye on her, which wouldn't have been such a bad job, if her attitude hadn't said she plainly detested him. So much for any girl being thrilled to meet him.

He sighed and took an abrupt turn rather than entering the Great Room. He had more important things to do than think about spoiled, moody princesses, namely checking with his scientists. It was going to be awfully difficult to reclaim what was rightfully theirs without his army of battle droids fully functional.

Chapter 5:

MEILIN - THE ROYAL SUITE

She didn't get far, servants kindly hustling her back into the Great Room, where she immediately noticed the Prince's absence. After the Empress sweetly said she hoped Meilin was feeling better, and Meilin pretended to apologize profusely for her silly weakness, the Empress pardoned her strange lapse and admitted that apparently the intel about a Rebel amongst the princess candidates had been wrong. Meilin made sure to express appropriate relief with the rest of the girls that none of them were vicious traitors.

They were then shown to their rooms to rest and freshen up before dinner. Meilin had thought they'd be together, in the same large suite of rooms, but instead she was shown to her own small, private suite. Finally alone, she collapsed onto the cushy, rich duvet.

If Grandmama had been the Empress Mother's long-lost cousin, she guessed that made her actual royalty of some sort. It was all too crazy. Her grandmother had always been a hardworking farmer. She and Grandpa had still shone with love for each other anytime Meilin had caught them in a moment alone. They had lived together with their family on the silk farm until their deaths just months apart when Meilin was twelve. She was glad they hadn't lived to see the plague sweep through their township and their family.

She remembered her grandmama particularly. Meilin had

learned to weave the finest crepe money could buy at Grandmama's knee. Her starts, stops, and errors were all skillfully sewn into
her own colorful holiday dresses, though most days they wore
homespun cotton like everyone else. She particularly remembered
a party dress that became her favorite girlhood play dress, even as
she outgrew it, with a multicolored pinealabra fruit design pieced
together from the scrap bin by Grandmama's skilled hands.

Though full of love for her and her parents, Grandmama
did always have an air about her—of secrecy. Now Meilin finally
knew why.

"Oh Grandmama," she sighed just before there was a knock
on the door. She groaned, rolled over and opened it to find a
bellhop delivering her battered suitcase. Her heart skipped a beat.

"Have they already unloaded the entire transport then?" she
asked with what she hoped was a merely curious tilt to her head.

"Oh no, Princess." The bellhop bowed. "It will take hours to
unload and inspect all of the cargo."

She thanked him and forced herself to close the door and
wait until he had to be out of sight. She needed to get to the cargo
bay before they unloaded the rocket. But, she opened the door
and nearly ran over a matronly woman and a familiar girl who
had to be a maid. Yun put a finger to her lips behind the woman's
back and Meilin quickly turned her attention to the woman who
stopped mid-knock and curtsied, like the bellhop had bowed—to
her! This day was getting stranger and stranger.

"Princess, may we come in?" the matronly woman bustled
in without Meilin's answer. She was an older woman, who would
have had grey hair had it not been shaved. Instead Meilin could

see grey stubble on her wrinkled scalp, and it sort of made her look like a hairless cat. "I am Mrs. Winstrol, and this is Yun, your lady's maid." She gestured to Yun, who Meilin almost hadn't recognize at first, having lost every bit of her hair down to the eyelashes.

"We are so very glad to have you with us. If there is anything you need, just ask one of us and we will do our best to make it happen. Now," she showed Meilin around the small suite, though she could very well see where the bathroom was and open the drawers for herself. Yun busied herself smoothing the wrinkles from the bed, not making eye contact and trying to hide a pleased smirk. She started unpacking Meilin's suitcase.

"Aren't any of the other girls rooming with me?" she asked. "I'd thought we were to share." And though the privacy might come in handy, she'd never had a room alone to herself.

"My dear," Mrs. Winstrol seemed aghast. "You're a Royal now, far more so than any of those girls. Why, this suite was kept ready for your grandmother, should she ever return."

"It was? Grandmama lived in the palace? Was it very full with extended family then?"

"I suppose it would have been, had the Empress Mother had any other cousins. But alas, no. They were raised as close as sisters, you know. It is said that the Empress Mother was devastated when Princess Ming-Yu ran off to Lyric with that accursed stable boy." She glared as if it was still an affront fifty years later.

"My grandfather you mean?" Meilin raised an eyebrow.

"Oh dear, forgive me. I'm sure he must have been an extraordinary man for the Princess to leave like that, with merely a note."

"He was. And they loved each other."

"Hmmm," Mrs. Winstrol refrained from saying anything more.

Another knock came at the door and Yun ran to open it before Meilin could. A handsome, older man with a shiny, smooth head, impeccable suit, and a measuring tape around his neck walked in, followed by a pretty young woman carrying a stool with a stack of multi-colored fabrics and a notepad on top.

The man took one look at Meilin and threw his arm dramatically over his eyes. "Ugh!" he said. "The Empress was right! You *are* wearing old rags, you poor thing! Where did you get this travesty of a dress?"

"Ummm…" She looked down at herself. It wasn't the greatest or newest dress ever, but the borrowed dress was certainly fancier than any she'd ever owned.

"Never mind, never mind. We'll get you all fixed up." He snapped his fingers at his assistant to put the stool in the middle of the floor and the materials on the bedspread. Then she gently took Meilin's arm with calloused fingertips. Meilin rolled her eyes but allowed herself to be led up onto the stool where he began taking every conceivable measurement, snapping them rapid fire at the girl to write down.

She immediately thought of the candies hiding in her pocket and hoped he didn't notice, but though he grunted and moved them to the side for her hip measurement, he didn't demand that she empty her pockets. He got to her chest measurement and said, "Breathe out." Instead, Meilin subtly breathed in as much air as she could hold. Dresses were bad enough, but no way was she going to assist in not being able to breathe.

When she could breathe normally again, she asked, "How do you like living in the palace? What is it like to work for the Empress?"

He started throwing material swatches over her shoulders, fluffing them around her neck. "Oh, it is the most marvelous place to live and work!" he gushed. "Ivory, yes. White, no," he said to his assistant. "The Empress is the most marvelous, stylish Empress who has ever lived, and she hires only the most talented and stylish designers." He puffed his chest. "Jewel tones, yes. Pastels, no."

"Hmm, I'm sure," she agreed, taking note of what little he'd said. The most marvelous, most stylish Empress. He might as well have said she had the personality of a toad.

He continued with swatch after swatch. She picked up one of the discarded pieces and ran it though her fingers. She grunted. The weave was sub-par and the silk worms had been allowed to mature too long, weakening the strands. Plus, she could detect tiny bits of debris actually woven *in*to the fabric. No wonder the Empress itched.

The tailor grunted as well. "Yes, we are currently in search of a new silk manufacturer. Our previous source on Lyric just up and stopped producing several years ago. It's a pity."

You mean the farm burned to the ground, Meilin corrected mentally, but worked to keep her expression neutral.

"Especially since they also produced the Empress's favorite sweet. We have been struggling to find other producers of equal quality, but none are quite as good. I guess that's what we get for relying on one producer for so long."

Maybe that's what you get for cutting us off when we needed help the most, she thought. Her fingers sparked with anger and she clasped her hands together in the folds of her dress, taking a deep, calming breath.

"What was that?" The tailor asked, rocking back on his feet.

"Oh dear, I believe I must have picked up some static electricity walking on this lovely rug. I admit I was enjoying rubbing my toes into it."

"Ah, yes. You have nice taste, Princess." He returned to checking colors against her skin and hair.

"Bright coral—"

"No. No pink," Meilin said.

"Are you sure? I have a lovely new—"

"No," she cut him off again. "No pink."

He considered her. "No pink or coral," he conceded, as if they were separate colors. "Purple?" He checked the swatch against her skin and shuddered. "No, no purple." He made sure the seamstress marked it down.

She shrugged a shoulder. "And the Prince?" she found herself asking, though she didn't know why. "What is he like?"

The tailor sniffed. "The Prince is a Warrior, like his father before him, God rest the Emperor."

"God rest the Emperor," the others murmured.

"But he has none of his mother's sense of timing or style."

She heard the tailor's reply, but watched the young seamstress in the mirror. She didn't start in fear or wince at the question, she merely looked up from her notes, smiled reassuringly, and said,

"He is a good Prince. Kind." Fine. Maybe she could let him live. They'd have to wait and see.

"Well of course he is," said Mrs. Winstrol sharply. "We have the finest, most resplendent Empress and Prince that ever ruled. You shall never hear one word against either of them."

"Of course not," Meilin murmured, except from those of us who want them dead.

Chapter 6:

MEILIN - DINNER WITH THE EMPRESS AND PRINCE

She found herself at dinner that night at the center of the table, flanked by her *favorite* people, Celestine and Kaletra, and across from the Prince and the Empress. She ignored them, intending to savor every morsel of the beef medallions in a rich brown sauce set in front of her. Rice grew poorly on Lyric, but the creamy mashed potatoes sprinkled with herbs reminded her of the insides of the fried silkworms they'd eaten back on the farm. Nutritious and delicious.

She tasted a bite of the tender beef, nearly groaning in ecstasy. It was better than anything she'd ever tasted. Beef was a luxury even on Lyric, but here… she mentally shook her head. But surely they couldn't keep cattle here on the moon, or grow the copious amounts of feed they needed. Not moon, The *Jewel* of Gallaius, she corrected herself. But crusting a rock in gold leaf did not make it a jewel.

She looked down the table and caught Imogen's eye. "Oh my God!" Meilin mouthed to her, rolling her eyes in pleasure at the meal in front of them.

"Oh my God, you!" Imogen mouthed back, pointing at Meilin. She just shrugged in bewilderment at her sudden change in status.

The Empress cleared her throat loudly and gave the two of them the stink eye before returning to her own conversation with the advisor next to her. Meilin guessed that princesses were above all to be silent. She overheard the Empress asking if they'd had any luck finding the maker of "those wonderful candies brought by Governor Fong." The advisor shook his head.

"Well someone must make them!" she exclaimed. "I don't care if Governor Fong doesn't remember. Search them out! And what about a new silk maker? Surely someone, somewhere can produce decent silk for me."

The advisor told her they were doing their best, but the silk-worms kept dying at the new farms, and whatever notes there had been on silk production from her favorite producer had not survived the fire. Without access to the original Terran records, either from war-torn Earth which had been out of communications for decades, or from the destroyed libraries of planet Gallaius, they were missing some of the finer points in silk production.

Meilin disguised a snort of dark amusement as a sneeze and seized another bite of beef. Of course the worms kept dying. She'd burned the mulberry trees and her grandfather's notebooks to ash before leaving. She looked up to find the Prince watching her from across the wide table. He raised an eyebrow and his wineglass at her. In return, she saluted him with her chopsticks holding a large slice of frivolous beef and stuffed it in her mouth, closing her eyes at the rich delicacy.

When she opened them again, he'd turned to talk to the girl next to him.

Meilin sighed and looked out the window. This one was also carefully draped against the view of the planet, but she could see various transports, many of them quite dirty, travelling back and forth between the moon and the planet's surface. What were they doing? She'd thought Gallaius was still dangerously irradiated.

Throughout dinner, and a gorgeous dessert of steamed pear encased in an ethereal cage of golden spun sugar, she noticed the other girls merely picking at their meals. No doubt trying to stay thin for the wedding day each of them was hoping to have. As for Meilin, she knew there'd be no wedding day for any of them if she did her job correctly, and that was fine by her. The Royals had ruined her happiness, killed her parents, and stolen their land. She only hoped she would soon be able to return the favor.

Chapter 7:

MEILIN - UNLOADING THE ROCKET

After dinner, Meilin was shown back to her room, in case she'd forgotten the way already. She was so stuffed she felt like she waddled, but as soon as she got there, she snuck out again and down the hall. She really had to get back to the shuttle bay. She'd only gotten a few *click-clacking* paces before taking off her borrowed but stylish heels. Still, she hadn't gotten far when she heard doors open and giggling behind her.

"Psst! Psssst! Meilin! Princess!" Several other girls ran on tiptoe to catch up with her. She hadn't realized she'd been trying to sneak past their rooms or she would've taken a different route. It was Orencia who'd spotted her—again. That girl had a nose for sneaking.

"Where are you going?" one of them asked with a giggle. "Not off to see the Prince already, are you?"

Meilin snorted. "No." But maybe they could help provide some cover. "I'm going to see the offloading, if we haven't already missed it. Wanna come?"

"The offloading?" one girl asked.

"Of the rocket?" this whisper was excited. Meilin nodded. "Yes!"

"Count me in!"

Meilin winced and held two fingers to her lips. If they weren't caught, it'd be a miracle.

A gaggle of princesses were about as quiet as an elerinoppo

in a glass blower's shop, but they made it to the shuttle bay in time to see the final offloading of their ship. It was a relatively large ship for having only fifteen passengers, because most of its cargo had been other things. Foods in quick freeze units and fresh produce in refrigerators, furniture and rugs in rich colors and gilded gold, all ready for the palace. She spotted piles of rich fabrics, the softest of furs from the finest bunneluffelump farmers on Lyric, already dyed a rainbow of colors and sparkling with imbedded jewels. There were pallets of beautiful blonde and dark woods, ready for assembly into a stunning gazebo for the Prince and his chosen princess, and boxes marked "Delicate!" with pictures of star-shaped glass luminaries. Hairless mole-rat footmen inspected each crate and carried them straight to the Empress's storage rooms. There were even cages of glorious exotic birds headed either for the Empress's aviary, or her table, Meilin wasn't sure which. That explained the strange noises in the night during transport—and the smell. So that hadn't been Celestine's attitude after all.

Speaking of whom, there she was, watching from the side and directing the footmen with Kaletra at her side.

"That simply must, must, must go on top!" she cried, pointing at a heavy, sturdy wooden crate that almost certainly should go on the bottom of any stack of goods. "I've seen them myself, the most gorgeous hand-blown, and above all, delicate glass lights you've ever seen. If any one piece were crushed or broken, why…" she stopped her rant, with her hand at her throat, too aghast to even think of such a tragedy.

The head footman sighed. "We will carry it alone, as if our

lives depended on it, Princess."

"And make sure nothing is stacked atop it!" Kaletra echoed shrilly. The footmen bowed to their two volunteer "helpers" and carried it away to the inspector, who was backed up, with at least twenty cases lined up for him to look through. And at last came the piece they'd all been waiting for, a large antique rocket ship that had been so carefully packed aboard the transport that it couldn't even be touched during shipping. Meilin knew, as she'd tried to get to it several times during transit from Lyric with no luck.

It was wrapped in several layers of bubble-stick and encased in a large wooden frame. The head footman wanted to move it out of the way, directly into a storage room so they could stack the other non-perishables around it. But the inspector was being nothing if not thorough in his work.

"I insist we unwrap and inspect it here, immediately. This, thing, is only listed on the manifest as 'firework rocket, engagement present for the Prince and his Princess from Governor Fong." He glanced at Celestine before continuing in a more conciliatory tone. "That tells me it has explosives inside that may have shifted during transit. I must inspect it for safety here, along with all the rest of these crates before you move any of it into the Palace."

The footmen gave in and began cutting the wrap off the rocket, while the head footman tried to insist that the girls leave during the inspection for safety. "It's a rocket packed with fireworks, after all. It could explode at any minute." But Celestine and Kaletra led the way in demanding they be allowed to stay.

Meilin didn't pay attention to their arguments but watched the rocket, and her mission, emerge.

"Oh!" the girls exclaimed as the wrap fell away. "Isn't it beautiful!" And it was. The vintage rocket had a brand-new paint job of metallic swirls and firework explosions set against Lyric's deep, velvety purple night sky. Each exploding firework was studded with hundreds of tiny gemstones that added an additional level of luxurious sparkle. Because nothing said wealth like literally lighting something expensive on fire and cheering as it blew up.

Celestine glowed as if every compliment the girls heaped upon the rocket was for her own work. Really, it was her father's present to the Prince and, presumably his daughter, on their engagement. Her pride made her even more demanding, if possible.

"It is not merely an entertainment! It is also a resplendent decoration. It must be hung carefully, in full view of the Royal court before and during the engagement party."

While the head footman tried to placate Celestine and keep her back at the same time, the inspector ignored her and focused on gently getting the hatch door open. He grunted and proceeded to carefully open the old hatch door. He sighed in relief when it didn't immediately explode.

The inspection seemed to take forever and Meilin hoped her colleagues with the Rebellion had done their jobs well in hiding the rocket's true capabilities. He opened every panel and tap-*tapped* every wall inside and out, looking for hidden compartments. But finally he was satisfied, exited, and replaced the hatch door.

"It seems to be in order, and exactly what it says," he announced. "An elaborate fireworks display contained within a rocket body. There are even instructions inside on how and when to fire it. Everything seems correct and in order."

"Well, of course it does! My father had it made for m-, I mean, the Prince's engagement party. He says so in his letter included with the manifest, if you'd bothered to read it," Celestine huffed, affronted by the doubt expressed by such a thorough inspection. She stomped out and the rest of the girls followed.

Chapter 8:

MEILIN - BREAKFAST WITH THE PRINCESSES

The next morning, Yun woke her much too early, bustling her into a hot shower and a robe before sitting her down to do her hair and makeup. Meilin tried explaining that she usually didn't go to that much trouble, but Yun was having none of it.

"You mustn't be over confident! You still have to compete for the Prince's hand and you need to look your best," she said, pulling beauty products out of a large basket before dabbing, daubing, and eyelash curling. A knock came at the door and Yun ran to answer it. The seamstress from the night before was delivering a new dress, underclothes, and a new pair of torture shoes. Joy.

Meilin looked at the girl's drawn face. "You look exhausted. Did you stay up all night sewing?"

The dress was a lovely black and cream print with a wide cream collar. It was relatively simple, except for a giant, coral bow on one shoulder.

"Yes, and you have more coming. Do you like it?" she asked eagerly.

She would rather wear pants with unrestricted movement but, "Um… It's lovely," Meilin sighed. She fingered the bow and wondered how well it was attached.

The girl grinned. "Wait." She unhooked the bow from a hidden clasp. "There. I knew that bow was going to have to go, but the tailor insisted."

"Whew, thank you. Now it really is lovely. You did a wonderful job." The seamstress blushed and curtsied. Just then, another young woman was shown in, who held at least three more dresses, all in shades of pink, peach, and coral.

"Um," Meilin began.

"Don't worry, these are for some of the other girls." The head seamstress grinned, making her way to the door where the other girl waited.

"Oh, whew. You did all these in one night? Wow."

"Well, I had help," she said modestly.

"Still, I'm impressed. Grandmama was fast, but not that fast."

"You mean, the lost Princess was a seamstress?" she asked eagerly.

Meilin nodded and the girl beamed. "Mrs. Winstrol asked me to tell you and the other Princesses that breakfast will be in the dining room in fifteen minutes, and not to be late."

"Oh my! We had better hurry!" Yun exclaimed and the others saw themselves out while Yun poked and prodded Meilin into the new, starched underclothes and dress. It wasn't terrible, but that tailor had obviously seen her breathe in during her measurements because the bodice was tight. Boob lifting tight. She looked at herself in the full-length mirror after Yun helped her into the shoes.

"Oh, look at you!" Yun said. "I'm starting to believe we might even pull this off," she added under her breath. As Meilin's Rebel support, one of Yun's first tasks had been to sweep the room for listening devices, but she still seemed paranoid about being over-heard saying anything Rebel-ish.

"I feel like a doll," Meilin said, making a face, to which Yun merely laughed darkly and ushered her out the door.

Breakfast at the palace was at least less formal than dinner, seeing as the Prince and Empress were elsewhere for the meal. Meilin sat with Imogen and her new roomie Orencia, a wide-eyed girl of eighteen who made Meilin feel old at twenty-three.

"So," Imogen said. "You're a real Princess now. Is that crazy or what? How did you not know?"

Meilin shrugged. "Grandmama and Grandpa didn't tell anyone."

"Oh, that's so romantic!" Orencia gushed. "Were they very in love?"

Meilin nodded and couldn't help but smile, remembering the joy they'd found in each other, and in their family, like every moment they'd fought for was precious. *And the ex-Princess and her ex-stableboy began their new life together, and yes, they lived happily ever after.*

Someday maybe… but no. Happily ever after was not in Meilin's future.

"I guess that makes you the front runner for the Prince's hand, doesn't it?" another voice asked dryly.

Meilin shrugged, looking around to see all the girls at the table leaning in their direction.

"You're soooo lucky," another girl chimed in from down the table. "He's dreamy!" Half the girls sighed.

"Nah, marrying the Prince is not in my plans. He's all yours," Meilin said.

"What?" several girls gasped. "Then why did you come?"

"Wasn't really a choice, was it?" Meilin said.

"What *are* your plans then?" Celestine sneered from the other end of the table.

Meilin raised a haughty eyebrow back. "World domination."

The girls laughed while Celestine huffed and rolled her eyes.

After Meilin ate her food, a savory mash topped with a soft-boiled egg and sliced green onions, and the other girls picked at theirs, Mrs. Winstrol ushered them out for a tour. They walked the palace, hearing about this Emperor or that Empress pictured in old paintings hung in the marble corridors, and Meilin wished for more black tea.

Chapter 9:

MEILIN - A TOUR WITH THE PRINCE

She debated sneaking away and exploring on her own when they were led down some stairs, to an under-palace transport line where a gleaming tram was waiting for them. They piled aboard and when they were all seated, chatting about the splendor of the palace (and its hunky Prince) who then climbed aboard, but the Prince himself. All chatter stopped.

"Ladies," he bent in a small bow. "The Empress has asked me to join you for a tour of the Jewel of Gallaius." His expression hid impatience at this news, but he seemed to be trying to be gallant about it.

The palace event planner moved over for him to take her spot up front, presumably for him to give the tour, but instead he sat, a few rows in front of Meilin, taking up an entire bench seat so no one would try to sit with him. She rolled her eyes.

"But the Empress said—" the planner began.

"I promised Mother that I would go on this tour with the lovely princess candidates, and here I am. But we both know you are better equipped to be our guide." He made a lazy rolling motion with his hand. "Please proceed."

"But," she pressed her lips into a thin line, obviously unhappy as he unhooked his com from his wrist and flicked it out to unfurl and stiffen into a thin, book-sized com pad.

"I am sure you will do a most admirable job," he said and with that, he gave the device his complete attention.

"Very well," she said and began the tour. "Princesses, please feel free to ask any and all questions you may have about our beautiful home, the Jewel of Gallaius," she recovered with a gallant flourish.

That was the wrong thing to say. Meilin was glad she'd sat at the back as the girls started peppering her with questions, hoping to impress the Prince, though he was not paying them one iota of attention. She caught a glimpse of his screen and saw dirty, antique wheeled vehicles zooming around a foliage rich landscape. His long fingers moved rapidly over the bottom of the screen and every once in a while, he put one finger to his ear as if listening. Was he playing some sort of game? Ugh.

The tram rose out of the palace and soon they were travelling through a clear glass tube high above the surface. Meilin looked down to see the gleaming palace, and the walled-off military compound side by side under the central and oldest dome. Newer domes attached like spokes on a wheel atop the dusty moon surface. The clear tube they rode through ducked into and back out of the shining domes like a clear snake that regurgitated people at various destinations.

"How does this train run, do you know?" Orencia asked quietly next to her. "There are no rails in this tube."

"Electro-magnets," Meilin answered automatically. She could feel their thrum through her whole body. It was invigorating, better than the tea she'd been wishing for, but she was looking out the window at Gallaius. Transport ships buzzed like bees back and forth from the planet's surface to the moon and into various air-lock doors in the Jewel's glass domes.

"Precisely," their guide said, clapping her hands together. "I am impressed." She glanced at the Prince to see if he was impressed too, but his attention was on his com pad. Her smile was tight when she looked back at Meilin. "You must be a student of Jewelian technologies."

"Not really," Meilin replied.

The woman sighed and turned back to the others. Meilin looked back to the Prince's com pad. The scene had not changed much, and the game was ridiculous. Why would anyone use vehicles so inefficient that they belched out black smoke like that?

But the Prince caught her looking over his shoulder and turned so his back was to the window and his com pad turned away from everyone. What he didn't seem to realize was that his screen was now reflecting on the window past his shoulder, and Meilin continued to watch.

The dirty, antique road vehicles were chasing something, a white shuttle that looked like the ones currently buzzing back and forth between the moon and Gallaius. The Prince tensed and swore under his breath.

"We are now entering our agricultural dome." Their guide glanced at the Prince in apparent alarm, but continued. "We raise fresh crops and a few animals here for the Palace. The rest of our food, as you probably know, is brought in from Lyric."

"How do you grow anything in this soil?" one of the girls asked. Their guide covered her surprise with a delighted smile. Yes, Meilin thought, several of these girls *do* come from the farms that provide food to your desolate moon.

"Yes, it's true the moon's soil is poor," she answered. "So we mine soil, among other things, from the planet." That explained the ships but…. Come on, wasn't anyone going to ask the obvious question?

Meilin sighed and spoke up, still distracted by the chase scene reflecting on the window. "But isn't it all still radiated down there?" The dirty wheeled vehicles were gaining on the shuttle, which was barely skimming above the ground. Why didn't it take off?

"Oh, the rad levels are much better seventy years later than predicted. The ozone has almost completely repaired itself. Plus, when I say we mine for soil, what I mean is that we scrape away the top layer, down to soil with no more than the typical radiation from the sun. We mix that with our moon soil and other amendments and it grows crops quite well, with added moisture of course."

"And the water?" Another girl asked. "Does that all get shipped in too?"

"No, it's done in our air and water plant. I don't quite know how it works, to tell the truth, except that they used to mine underground ice deposits here on the Jewel, but now it's much less expensive to manufacture water."

"They must bring in hydrogen and oxygen from the planet," Imogen said next to Meilin, "which of course, is also necessary for the air we're breathing. They combine the two in a lab and the reaction, besides producing water, also produces energy, which they store in tuotarium crystals that power everything, the dome, the palace, this tram, when the Jewel's solar grids are out of range of the sun."

"Yes, yes that's right, princess Imogen. Where did you learn all of that?" the guide said in wonder.

As much as Meilin was wondering the same thing, she had to hold herself back from snapping at the woman for underestimating her new friend. Imogen merely smiled calmly and said, "I've just finished my medical degree, and I've always enjoyed chemistry and physics. I was just starting work at our hospital when I got the call that I was requested here."

"Hmm, yes, and one does not deny the Empress's request," the guide muttered with a smile plastered across her face.

Meilin went back to watching the window. Tuotarium crystals efficiently stored energy for vehicles, and never produced smoke. Were they supposedly burning natural resources straight out of the planet's crust? What kind of uneducated barbarians - and then she (mentally) smacked her forehead. That's who the Prince was watching. The Barbarians on Gallaius. Watching, not playing. They were really chasing a mining vessel.

And when he pressed his finger to one ear like he was now, he had to be listening to some sort of rescue effort. His fingers moving across the screen must be asking more information or giving orders, since he couldn't give them verbally with delicate princesses around. The mining vessel had to be damaged and having trouble escaping.

What she saw next was a barbarian leaning out the side of his speeding, bumping vehicle, mud flying from the outsized tires. He was all long, flying hair with dark goggles covering his eyes. He aimed a surprisingly elegant-looking weapon with a silver nose cone at the mining vehicle and in seconds, it dropped from its hover straight down to the ground, completely dark now and motionless. The antique vehicles slid to a stop in the marsh and barbarians jumped out to surround the miners.

She could see that some of the barbarians had long, matted hair like their leader, while others were bald, with black tattoos over their scalps. She wished she could see them better. As if in answer, Prince Cor zoomed in on the man in front, holding the weapon, and the man's stats appeared next to him:

SKOLE

OLDEST KNOWN BARBARIAN AND COMMANDER

~40 YEARS. 250 LBS. 6'2"

RAD LEVEL: HIGH

WEAPONS: PRIMITIVE BLADE WEAPONS OF ALL KINDS. SKILLED SWORD FIGHTER. UPDATE: EMP WEAPON.

The graciously curved blaster that this Skole held looked like it had been white at one time, but had been rolling around in a swamp along with its owner.

He was big and looked older than forty, with a muscular girth that spoke of a high protein diet. He had matted hair and looked like he didn't know the word bath, or toothbrush. A few of his men were as big as he was, though most looked shorter, scrawnier, and much younger.

They quickly surrounded the dead mining transport, two men running up to either side of the door with big, forked pry bars, bringing the ramp door down. Prince Cor seemed to be holding his breath, and Meilin found herself doing the same. The silence from the muted video made the wait for the door to fall even more tense.

Finally, the transport door came down and out sprang a half-dozen warriors of the Royal Guard in white helmets and pristine grey body armor. The lead barbarian grinned at first, firing expanding waves of blue charged energy at the guards. But instead of carrying the compact blasters she was accustomed to seeing in footage of the Royal Guard, they carried long, thin double-handed swords in the old style called *miaodao*. The barbarian's smile fell away as his energy weapon had no effect. He threw it aside and pulled a giant, wicked looking sword from a sheath on his back. The backside of the pitted, black blade sported jagged spikes and serrations that looked as though they'd tear a man to shreds with one swipe.

But where the barbarians and their weapons seemed designed with size and intimidation in mind, the guards with their old-style *miaodao* were elegant and efficient, with precise, practiced movements. They leapt at the nearest barbarians, slicing down the first few with ease and the junior barbarians fell quickly with silent, lethal blows. As they lay dying, their leader made his escape, scooping up the directed energy weapon as he fled to his vehicle. She could almost hear the roar as it belched black pollution and sped away, leaving the dead barbarians and the mining shuttle stranded in the swamp.

"No! Agh! He's getting away!" Prince Cor exclaimed, looking about to tear his short hair out, then looked up as the princess candidates turned to stare at his outburst. He swallowed, then smiled with what Meilin was coming to realize was fake charm. He shrugged. "My favorite team, the Titans, just lost the ball and the match. My apologies, ladies, but it couldn't be missed."

The girls, immediately forgave his preoccupation and twittered consolation. When he glanced her way though, Meilin had a hard time pasting a believable smile on her face. She had been briefed on the Jewel's weapons capabilities and she definitely did not recall a directed energy weapon capable of knocking transports out of the sky. So, either the barbarians were much more technologically advanced than they looked, or the Prince had somehow lost a newly developed weapon to the barbarians. And it had been turned against his fleet. Now apparently, they were having to manually guard mining ships with soldiers and swords, instead of blasters and drones while the Prince watched in luxury from afar. Charming.

The other girls had been too polite to stare at what he'd been watching, but several probably knew that it hadn't been sports. However, Meilin was probably the only one to know the truth. He went back to his admirers and Meilin went back to staring out the tram window, lost in thought about this new revelation, both of the Jewel's potential fire power, and the threat of the barbarians.

The Prince quickly voiced an excuse and got off at the military complex, oozing with pseudo-charm. Meilin could see guards at a guard station, waiting to turn back wayward princesses she supposed. Soldiers, male and female, walked around in boring fatigues and she wished she were among them. That's what she'd trained for. Instead, she was here, in fancy dresses and idiotic heels. She needed some exercise. And she needed to find a way to see the capabilities stored in that military complex.

Instead, they returned to the palace where Mrs. Winstrol announced they would be attending their first Royal etiquette class *with the Empress!* Meilin barely kept herself from rolling her eyes. On the other hand, perhaps this might be her opportunity to slip the Empress the candies.

Chapter 10:

MEILIN - ETIQUETTE CLASS GOES BADLY

Was it time? Was it finally time to slip the Empress her just desserts? Meilin laughed with the other girls in the Empress's elaborate tea room at something the Empress's social attaché had said. The Empress would be joining them shortly. Meilin fingered the fabric bag of individually wrapped golden mulberry sweets in her pocket, made, wrapped, and indistinguishable from the Empress's old favorite, except for one little addition. The Empress wouldn't even know she'd been poisoned until she was on the floor and it was too late, that murdering, medicine withholding witch.

There was an empty glass candy dish near Meilin on the sideboard. If she just had a little diversion, she could slip some in it. She put her hand into her pocket and pulled a few out of the pouch before moving to stand against the grand piece of furniture. She was moving her hand toward the glass dish when Orencia came to stand next to her, bumping her companionably. Now was her chance, behind Orencia's back, but… What if she or one of the other girls ate one? Meilin sighed and put the deadly golden gems back in her pocket.

It wasn't part of her mission, she reminded herself. It would tip their hand if the Empress was suddenly poisoned, but oh… it was so tempting.

"You look so serious," Orencia whispered. "Smile or someone might think you were plotting something." Meilin looked at her sharply, then pasted a smile on her face, and tried to pay attention during their princess etiquette prep session with the Attaché. Her mission depended on not sticking out like a sore thumb. But she found herself drifting off into daydreams of revenge as the Empress's social assistant walked around the room, correcting posture.

When she came to Meilin, she poked her in the back, jerked her shoulders back and tapped her chin up so her teeth cracked together. Now she wished she'd paid even a little better attention to the etiquette lessons that had been offered on the transport from Lyric. She sighed.

"Where were you raised, a pig farm?" the woman asked, not seeming to care about Meilin's supposed Royalness now. Celestine snickered nearby, with her perfectly straight, aristocratic bearing. Meilin ground her teeth but didn't respond. The Empress's Attaché completely adjusted Meilin's posture from head to foot and she was left feeling like a poseur ballerina. She gave a sigh of relief when they were at last allowed to sit, only to have to stand again, and sit, and stand, sit and stand until they did it "correctly". The Attaché then adjusted their sitting posture, placing a delicate, blown eggshell between each of their backs and the backs of their chairs.

"Knees and ankles together, ladies! Glue them if you have to. No crossing your legs at the knee, girl! Unladylike!" She whacked the offending girl on the leg and her eggshell cracked audibly.

There was much adjusting as they all, except Celestine, moved their chairs to get close enough to hold a teacup and pretend to eat finger foods off empty plates while sitting perfectly straight, ankles crossed, cradling an egg between their back and the chair. Meilin deliberately leaned back.

"Oops!" she smiled at the girls around her and let the ridiculous shell drop. Meilin sighed and checked her com under the table. Now would surely be a good time for the Rebellion to move in. But no, nothing.

"You, you, and you!" The Attaché snapped and Meilin jerked her head up as her com was snatched out of her hands. "If you're going to be so rude as to have coms at the table, we might as well put them to good use." She not so gently placed the com on Meilin's head to balance. Meilin sighed and the other girls groaned, but placed their coms on their heads also.

"Ladies, the Empress," a doorman announced, two of them opening the ornate double doors with a flourish. A footman behind each of them, pulled their chairs out and swept the eggs away at the same time. Each girl stood and stepped behind her chair as the footman stepped away. They all curtsied to the Empress.

As Meilin dipped in the show of respect, her com went clattering onto the table, knocking over her empty cup and saucer and rattling the silver. She gave the attaché woman a look and put the com back atop her head. When she looked to the door, the Empress and Prince were both regarding her with eyebrows raised, though the Prince's face held a smirk of amusement too.

"You look ridiculous," the Empress snapped. Meilin took that as her cue to take her com off her head. Yeesh, these people. Celestine snickered again and Meilin resisted throwing her com like a frisbee at her face and breaking her nose. She was sure she could do it. Watching the blood drip down and ruin the front of her flouncy floof of a dress would totally be worth it.

She realized the Empress was talking with the Prince again, still half in and half out of the room. The Prince had his hand on her arm and was saying that something "couldn't wait." Meilin sighed in relief that their attention was no longer on her and went to sit back down. The Empress's assistant shook her head and waved her hands below her waist in a frantic no, no, no gesture. Meilin stood back at attention, though what difference it made, she couldn't tell. The Empress appeared to not even notice or care that they had to stand as long as she did.

Meilin's present Royal stance was close to coming to military attention. The shoulders weren't as far back, the feet were more ballet, with one foot slightly forward, and toes out, but it was close. To entertain herself, she moved between the two positions while waiting. She found the Prince again staring at her with one eyebrow raised. She bobbed a curtsy at him and went back to pretending to be a bored princess. He grimaced and went back to trying to convince his mother of something. Meilin struggled to hear and read lips.

"Supply them?" the Empress was asking incredulously.

"Yes, Mother, they are still our people, after all."

"Radiated barbarians are not our people, Cormorin. Why would we want to supply them?"

"They're not all barbarians, Mother!" He seemed frustrated and his older lieutenant took over.

"My Empress," he schmoozed. "Perhaps you could try to think of these non-barbarian Gallaians as… pre-colonists. They are fighting the barbarians, after all."

"Fighting them? For us?" the Empress asked.

He nodded with a smile that oozed charm.

"Hmmm. Cormorin," she said imperiously, turning back to her son.

"Yes, Mother?"

"You may supply and train these," she waved her hand around, "pre-colonists to fight the barbarians, as long as they prove loyal to the Crown."

He sighed and seemed to restrain himself from rolling his eyes out of his head. "Yes, Mother."

"Excellent, my Empress." Cor's lieutenant bowed and they walked out.

Meilin pulled her eyebrows down out of her hairline and realized she could have used the masterful performance to slip the candies into the glass candy dish. She mentally kicked herself as the Empress turned back to the room full of princess candidates.

"Empress, Ladies," a servant announced grandly. "Tea is served."

And Meilin wondered if, between the Prince and his lieutenant, they could get the Empress to agree to just about anything.

An hour later, Meilin looked down at her ruined dress as she stomped back to her suite. That Celestine was going to get what was coming to her. But first, Meilin had to get out of this joke of a garment and find some workout clothes. She took a detour and headed downstairs to the laundry.

Chapter 11:

CORMORIN - SPARRING

Prince Cormorin got out of yet another frustrating meeting with his mother about those gawd awful simpering princesses, in which she would not discuss more important matters, like dealing with the barbarians that were becoming more and more of a problem for his troops and his plans for returning Planet Gallaius to habitable farmland. That goal was necessary both for the Jewel, and the surviving, sane Gallaians they had recently discovered living there underground, uncomfortably close to the barbarian stronghold. But his mother seemed unwilling to look at the bigger picture of their relationship with the planet they orbited.

The Empress also avoided the topic of the Rebel militia gaining steam on colony planet Lyric, which was fanning the flames of unrest. The latest report from Governor Fong said the Rebels were encouraging Lyrans to not pay their tithe of goods and instead trade them on the growing black market, which was the last thing they needed as he tried to supply his forces on Gallaius and provide some relief to surviving Gallaians.

But all Mother wanted to talk about was her demand that Cor choose a bride. He'd gritted his teeth in frustration at her insistence that if they played this right, it would please their people and encourage loyalty. Cor doubted this would help much with any group other than their loyal base.

And now Mother was insisting that he go on a date with each girl, to be broadcast to the entire kingdom as a public relations

gambit. How was he supposed to act Royal and princely and admirable when it sounded like the most boring, useless chore he
could think of? He'd worked hard to eschew the vid crews of his
youth only for her to order them back to following him and these
new princesses too. He'd always hated being a living vid show.

He'd told his mother that she should go ahead, pick one of
them if she was so determined that he marry, but she had not
accepted that suggestion. She'd only unwrapped a candy that had
arrived in a present from Governor Fong and begun talking about
how lovely the Governor's daughter Celestine was. As far as he'd
seen, she was beautiful in a showy Royal kind of way, which was
probably what his mother liked about her, but he hadn't spent
enough time talking with her to determine if she possessed a
personality.

In fact, the only one he was sure about was that infuriat-
ing dark haired one who had turned out to be descended from
his grandmother's long-lost cousin. *She* kept popping into his
thoughts at all inconvenient times. If the attitude she'd given him
was her idea of ass-kissing, he was interested to see what she
would do in front of a vid crew.

He stomped off to train some newly arrived recruits, bypassing security and stripping off his dress jacket as he went. His
scientists had better get that EMP shield they were working on
up and running for his ships and weaponry. He had a feeling he
was going to need them.

It seemed the barbarians wanted nothing more than to roar
around on their ancient, sooty vehicles, scavenging and raiding,
his mining and supply ships included. He was still pissed that

they'd managed to overtake and capture several of his transit ships and his directed EMP weapon. He knew they were still trying to figure out how to make the ships fly, but they'd definitely figured out how to fire the directed EMP and were causing problems for his troops and mining vessels. He needed that shield or his stock of drones and weaponry would be useless in taking out the barbarian stronghold with minimal casualties. Without it, well what he needed now was to hit something.

He walked into the training room and hung his jacket, and his shirt too, on a row of hooks by the door, and kicked off his sandals. His recruits were busy training in old-style mixed martial arts techniques. If their energy weapons were going to be taken off-line without warning by his own, stolen, EMP they had to be able to beat the barbarians hand-to-hand. At least the old-style black powder projectile weapons from Earth had never come to Gallaius in any significant quantity. The barbarians had long since run out of the projectiles needed for those antique weapons and were down to badly made swords that were none the less effective. His troops would have to fight hand-to-hand, and win.

On a mat in the corner, sparring with bo staffs, was one of his better lieutenants getting his butt handed to him by a slight figure with short, dark hair who he didn't recognize. He spotted a facial projection on her, which told him she was new, as they were not allowed on the Jewel. He was surprised no one had explained that to her. She spun away like a dervish and back in, sweeping the man's legs out before pouncing, wooden practice knife drawn and poking his chest over his heart. He was walking over, to congratulate and ask the new recruit's name, when he got a good look at her face as she grinned and helped the big guy up. Even under her anti-rec screen, he knew it was her.

"Princess!" he yelped in surprise, to his embarrassment. The other recruits around hurriedly bowed to him, then her. She looked at him in annoyance, dark eyes flashing. Obviously, she hadn't introduced herself.

"One stupid blood test doesn't make me a princess and I'll wipe the floor with anyone who keeps their head bowed to me," she snarled at them, indeed looking nothing like a princess.

They looked to their Prince, but straightened one by one.

"What are you doing here?" he asked. "Take that silly thing off your face, they're illegal on the Jewel. And where did you get those clothes?"

She sniffed and seemed to be trying not to look at his bare chest. "It's makeup, though apparently I ought to practice more. And, I needed some exercise. This blasted moon is making me soft."

He squinted at her. "So you just asked for a recruit's uniform and the maids brought you one without question? And then someone showed you into my training camp?"

"Of course not. I found the laundry. There was a whole pile."

"And they just let you have one?"

She gave him her haughtiest look yet. "They didn't see me."

"And here. No one stopped you from waltzing onto my military base?"

"Are you kidding? In these clothes, I belong here."

"Well, since you're here," he said through clenched teeth. "The Empress has ordered us on a date. Be ready in an hour."

Her eyes flared fire at his command, but he found he liked how the rounded parts of her moved beneath that plain shirt as her breathing sped up. Several of his recruits snickered and she glared around at them, shutting them up with a look. That was interesting.

And then she smiled that fake gracious smile of hers that he was coming to detest. "As romantic as that sounds, I have a better idea." She whirled and snatched the bo right out of his lieutenant's hands and threw it at him. "You beat me and I'll agree to a date with you. Easy, right?"

He merely grinned. He didn't think anything was going to be easy with her.

They began and he had to admit he was impressed. But that didn't mean he was going to hit her, at least not hard. He saw an opening to sweep her legs and took it, only to realize too late that she'd left the illusion of an opening on purpose. She jumped his staff and came down with a warrior's yell and her staff flat on his back, driving him to his knees. He rolled away, under her next spinning strike and back to his feet. She had guts, he'd give her that. Not many would try to take the Prince's head off.

"Impressive. Where did you learn?"

"Lyric, of course," she said, which told him precisely nothing.

"Who did you say your master was?"

"I didn't. Come on, hit me. Try at least." She blocked his combination of strikes and jabbed. He blocked in time to save himself a cracked rib or two, but he still wasn't going to hit her. They spun and swung, blocked and parried. Finally, they were both breathing hard and not getting anywhere. He spun his staff faster and faster in front of himself and backed away.

Meilin snorted with contempt, but accepted the draw. She'd also stopped really trying to hit him, obviously realizing he wasn't going to strike her no matter how many openings she left him. She turned and walked away.

He followed her to the door. "I don't hit ladies of the court," he said as she opened it and started to leave. "Wait, you're forgetting your shoes."

She gave him a withering look. "Those lifted torture devices? They would have given me away immediately." She walked out barefoot, as apparently she'd come.

Chapter 12:

MEILIN - CHEMISTRY, BUT NO DATE

Meilin heard Prince Cormorin sigh and come after her.

"It's a half mile back to the palace. Here, take my sandals," he said.

She glanced back to see him holding an overly large pair out to her. When she wouldn't take them, he sighed in exasperation and dropped them at her feet. He quickly lifted her against his bare chest without warning.

She caught her breath at the zing of electricity that moved between them and went still. She really should protest, but the feel of his skin on hers, his hard-muscled shoulders under her hands made her dumb. She looked up. His lips parted and his eyes dilated looking down at her. Damn, but she couldn't control the zip of electricity between them. He put her gently down into his giant, big-foot sandals. She was not going to be able to walk in those things without making a lot of slap, slap, slappy noises down the halls, but she somehow wasn't protesting, looking up into his dark eyes.

"I don't hit ladies," he repeated in a gruff voice. "It's a matter of respect."

"Respect?" she snapped, pushing away. Half the recruits in that training room were women, and she doubted he gave them a pass. She poked him in his over-muscled chest. "Do you know how close I was to getting on the other transport? I was almost one of your soldiers. It's what I trained for. But then, that ridiculous request came through for girls with 'Royal' blood to compete to be *your* bride and I was shoved into a dress and onto the losers' ship."

"Geez, tell me how you really feel." He ran a hand over his short, but real hair.

"All right. Royalty never did me one bit of good before and it certainly isn't helping me now. Respect used to be something I earned. Now it's based off a stupid blood test and how quietly I can sit and look pretty—for hours—all to impress some useless Prince. You want a date? There are fourteen other simpering idiots who would love to go."

With that, she whirled around and clomped away in his giant sandals, almost tripping on them. "Ugh!" She turned back and kicked them off, back at his shocked face. He ducked. Pity.

By the time she'd gotten back to her room, she was kicking herself. She didn't need him to like her, but she did need to be free to wander the palace grounds. Not only had she lost her trainee disguise the first time out, she was sure the guards would be on orders to watch for her and keep her away from the military base. And when the Empress heard about her refusal for a date with her son, there was a good chance she'd have her locked up in her gilded quarters until she changed her mind.

Well, she'd deal with that when she came to it, but she was going to have to come up with an alternate escape plan, just in case.

She quickly changed back into one of her new, already hated gowns and dreaded the update Yun was sure to send the Rebels.

Chapter 13:

MEILIN - THE PRINCE SENDS A GIFT

The next morning as she was getting ready for breakfast, there was a knock at the door. Yun grumpily opened it and came back with a delivery, a plainly wrapped package. There was a note on top that read:

Open in private.

She wished she could wait till she was alone, but after Meilin's mess-up the night before with the Prince, Yun was not about to leave without seeing what was in that package. Meilin opened it to find a set of practice fatigues and another note.

I still won't hit you. - Cor

She couldn't help the smile that spread across her face. After breakfast, she put on the new fatigues and sandals in her size and again snuck out of the palace. However this time, Yun insisted on going with her. When they walked into the military complex, the guards' attention was elsewhere and the two girls walked in seemingly unnoticed.

The second time the guards were looking the other direction as Meilin and Yun passed, she thought it was weird, too easy. The third time, she knew they'd been told to ignore her. It was almost as annoying as when the Prince had refused to hit her. The next day when Meilin and Yun went to work out, they took Orencia and Imogen with them, to test how far the Prince's misplaced graciousness would stretch.

It turned out, surprisingly, that Imogen and Orencia had both had pretty extensive martial arts training and were ecstatic at the chance to blow off some steam and kick the crap out of a heavy bag for a while. Maybe she shouldn't have underestimated them; they both had that ineffable self-confidence that said, *I can take care of myself.*

Meilin gave them some pointers and was delighted to find they could hold their own sparring the Prince's trainees. No one was more surprised than the trainees though, who looked at the princesses with a bit more respect after that.

The next morning Meilin found out that, in addition to Orencia being observant, she could not keep a secret to save her life. Four more princesses were waiting for Meilin and Yun.

Meilin had not seen the prince in several days, but when she came into the training room with half the princesses in tow in fatigues "borrowed" from the laundry, there he was with his troops, drilling them in sword mechanics. She couldn't help but watch the way his body moved through the positions, that is, until Yun elbowed her in the side with a huge eyeroll, saying "Come on."

Today, Meilin had decided to take the untrained princesses through a self-defense course with a little weapon she'd found a whole dusty box of in the training room, the micro-baton. Prince Cor and his trainees preferred traditional swords, but the micro-baton was an unassuming little metal rod, about five inches long and half an inch in diameter with grooves for a hand grip in the center, easily concealed and carried. She showed them how to hold it in their fists, using either end to punch, stab or jab an attacker in their soft spots or cause pain to hard, bony places. Meilin and Yun demonstrated some simple jabs and holds, Meilin being careful not to electrocute Yun. They then got the girls padded and paired up, and let them loose to practice.

Maddeningly, she kept catching herself looking at the Prince and once even caught him looking at her, she thought, as she worked with the girls, but he quickly turned away. But at least it wasn't just her. The other princess candidates were all distracted by the Prince being there, fluttering their lashes at him. But though he bowed in return when they caught his gaze, he didn't come over to talk with any of them, that is, until their training session was over and they were packing up to leave.

He walked toward Meilin, seeming to steel himself, taking a deep breath. She froze, watching him approach and her traitorous breath caught in her throat, until she realized he wasn't looking at her. He merely glanced at Meilin and nodded on his way past her to his objective. Meilin turned and saw Orencia frozen like a spot-lit gazellaphon. The younger girl took what seemed an involuntary step forward, as if stuck in his tractor beam gaze, and stepped on her micro-baton, rolling forward and flailing. Prince Cor quickly stepped forward and caught her gallantly.

He smiled, asked her if she was all right, and then asked her to accompany him to dinner that evening. Orencia, though red-cheeked with embarrassment, smiled and agreed, curtsying, and the girls watched him walk out of the training room, Meilin hearing multiple, audible sighs in his wake.

Meilin pasted on a smile and forced herself to join the girls in congratulating Orencia on being the first to get a date with the Prince. Orencia bustled out to get ready and Meilin went back to cleaning up, avoiding Yun's hawkish gaze. The rest of the girls invited Meilin, and Yun by extension, back to their suite to watch movies and gorge themselves on low-fat popcorn. Meilin declined, saying she was going to take a walk, leaving the princesses to their conclusion that she was upset about not getting the first date. She wasn't, at least she was trying not to be, but she did apparently need to get her head straight and remember why she was here. The rocket wouldn't be out of its burial in storage until the week before the Prince's engagement ball, so it was time to take this opportunity to explore the military base. Yun also declined the somewhat awkward invite, and excused herself back to her 'maid' duties.

She left her holo hair emitter atop her head, knowing it marked her as a princess in the Jewel's military compound and wondering how far they'd let her explore. How long would they assume her Royal blood meant she was also loyal? She activated the tiny camera atop her holo-hair emitter and set off into the heart of the compound, ready to play the part of a princess whose curiosity got the better of her if stopped.

She skirted the underground barracks, a few soldiers ignoring or nodding to her, but not questioning her. Only one barracks was full of new Lyran recruits, but one whole battalion seemed newly vacated. She overheard comments about being re-stationed on Gallaius, and she wondered what that meant. What sort of training could they get on radiated planet Gallaius that they couldn't get here?

She found more practice rooms, and then the armory. It was a cavernous underground bunker, filled with columns of soldier droids and military drones all lined up neatly, and armed with the newest in blaster tech. Along one wall hung additional rows of blasters of various types. And along another wall hung a selection of traditional swords, from the long, single-edged, two-handed *miaodao*, to the double-edged, single-handed *jian*, and more.

It was well known on Lyric that the Prince had been amassing this metal and silicone army for the better part of a year now. While the parts were manufactured on Lyric, and assembled here, there was no doubt what those parts built. And now, he was recruiting soldiers from Lyric too, and all the people of Lyric could do was speculate as to why.

The official reason was that the Royals were having trouble with some radiated barbarians on Gallaius. But Lyrans knew that the Royals had this whole metal army that Meilin saw spread before her now. So, why send for poor Lyran soldiers? The only reason the people of Lyric could come to was that the Prince was removing Lyric's ability to fight back when the time came. And that was why the Rebels had to strike soon. As soon as she got back to her room, she'd hand over the footage to Yun to work her magic in getting it to the Rebels.

But Meilin was troubled as she walked back. The Prince didn't seem like a person plotting war with Lyric, did he? And she couldn't help but remember the vid she saw on Prince Cor's com pad during their tour, of the barbarian with the stolen EMP blaster on Gallaius. She wished she'd been able to record that. But all she could do now was remind the Rebels of what she'd seen.

Over the next week and a half, Meilin had to tell herself repeatedly that she was not miffed. Not at all. She didn't want that arrogant Prince asking her out again anyway. Just because he was now asking out every princess candidate *but* Meilin was not cause for jealousy. She had turned *him* down first. But when those girls came back from their dates all glowy and swoony-eyed, every time! Well, she couldn't help but wonder....

No. Even if maybe, *possibly* he wasn't so bad—as her hormones kept arguing—his mother was. Meilin still carried the golden candies around daily, either in a pocket, or a waist pouch at the small of her back, waiting for the right opening to slip them to the Empress, though she had to admit, the wrappers were becoming a bit worn looking. Maybe if the lighting was dim.... Was there a Royal movie night coming up?

The thought made her scowl, again. Not unless you counted the Prince's romantic date nights. She'd seen the footage; his dates had been all over the Royal News. And what was worse, the Empress had sent a vid crew along on each and every outing, and she'd given permission for them to interview the princesses. The Empress was so desperate for good PR, both on the Jewel and on Lyric, where she couldn't ignore the growing Rebel sentiment, that she had authorized a vid show, "Princess Countdown".

Prince Cor had been on his best, most charming behavior. Pulling out the Princesses' chairs, ordering lovely meals on snowy linens, out on the starlit terrace, or a perfect picnic in the (filtered) sunlight of the Aviary. He kissed their cheeks at just the right moment, making the girls blush and giggle. He took several of the girls to the small farm to see baby goats, or to a theater production put on by the children of the workers who lived on the Jewel. Each date was perfectly planned and suited to each girl (according to the survey they'd all filled out prior to arrival). She reminded herself that the Prince only had to show up. The Royal Planner had done all the actual work.

Celestine had been particularly smug when she got a date before Meilin, but she reminded herself that she had bigger goals than a date with that disagreeable, smug, sexy prince. Though she did wonder what they would do. In unguarded moments, she had a few ideas.... She shook off the budding daydream. It was time to get that rocket operational.

Chapter 14:

MEILIN - THE ROCKET

They were finally going to hang the rocket at the center of the two-story Great Room for the entire two weeks before the Prince's announcement at his engagement ball.

The girls wouldn't know beforehand which of them would be chosen. They all had to dress up in ball gowns and wonder who he would choose, if it might just be her name that he called....

It was "all so dramatic" according to Kaletra. But Meilin knew it was all just a big PR ploy for the Royals. Giant waste of all the tithe money and goods from Lyric, but, hey, at least they would make an entertaining vid show.

Meilin snuck up to the second-floor balcony of the Great Room. Cushy benches sat along the walls, under rich paintings by long forgotten masters. The rocket was laying on its side next to the railing, taking up most of the space on the balcony itself. She stood up on her toes and grasped the door handle.

It was the middle of the night in the palace, though that was hard to tell from looking out the windows that lined the atrium and arced overhead, showing the palace dome and infinite space as they always did. It would be a spectacular spot for the shiny, painted rocket to hang, she had to admit. Facing the windows in her night dress, standing at the rail, she could almost imagine she was floating through space. All around her was deep black, studded with brilliant stars, and Gallaius off to one side, about to rotate out of view for the night and early morning. The curtains would cover it again when the Empress was present.

If caught by the guards, Meilin was ready to claim insomnia. But they had already passed this way on their usual rounds and she had ten minutes with the rocket if they continued their usual pattern.

She looked around once more and slipped the screwdriver and flashlight out of her night dress that she'd swiped earlier from a maintenance man's bucket. She made quick work of the screws that made sure no one opened the rocket before it was time, and opened the door down, toward the floor. She was climbing in when she heard it, a giggle, a mumbled, "Mmmm", and stumbling feet coming her way.

"Shinse," she cursed under her breath. It was too late to climb out and screw the panel back shut. She finished clambering inside and hauled the heavy door up by its interior strap and held it closed.

She heard fumbling and mumbling and half-drunken laughter, the sounds of a palace tryst?

"Shhh, you'll get me caught, *Lihwa*," an accented male voice whispered the word for princess.

"Oh hush. You like the excitement as much as I do," a female voice answered. A familiar voice. Celestine and the guard she'd been flirting with all week, she'd bet. Meilin continued to hold the door strap firmly wrapped around one hand while she turned on her flashlight with the other. As expected, the old rocket's lights were no longer functioning. She looked around in the overly bright beam making a spotlight surrounded by black in the small space. Outside, the kissing noises continued.

There were stacks of paper wrapped cylinders, wired neatly to the central control panel, looking like bombs to her. How the inspector had known it was only fireworks, she had no idea. Though fireworks did explode when lit. Maybe he'd just gone by the note on the door, which read:

To Operate Fireworks Display:

1) Aim rocket out airlock, into space - very important! Path must be clear!

2) Clear area! Extreme caution must be taken!

3) Push power button to launch. Rocket will fire after a five-minute delay. Do not, for any reason, alter wiring.

4) Close door panel. Latch shut. Vacate area.

5) Caution! Keep clear! Anyone in vicinity of rocket when it fires will suffer horrible, painful, burning death!

Well, that was clear enough.

Below was a description:

When rocket has traveled off the moon's surface into space, it will open, flower-like and produce fireworks.

Meilin turned her flashlight and attention toward the control panel, just as there was a *thump* on the rocket outside. She gasped and made sure the panel was still closed. It hadn't moved.

"Is this what you brought me to see, *Lihwa*?" the man outside asked.

Meilin heard more kissing noises and a moan. The rocket rocked a bit. She clapped the back of her hand with the flashlight to her mouth to hold in a laugh. The rocket moved again. They were really getting into it out there. She held her laughter and tried to concentrate on the task at hand, even as she had to brace her feet against the rocking.

She spotted a large red recessed button labeled: POWER.

Meilin avoided the button—no need to give the love birds outside a *real* thrill—and stuck the flashlight between her knees. She reached her hand toward the control panel.

"So much fabric. Why is there so much fabric?" She heard the guard complain. The rocket gave a big shake and they both moaned at the same time. Meilin tried to ignore them and concentrate. This was her big chance, her only chance before the rocket would be hung on display and out of reach, unless she wanted to perform some serious acrobatics.

She took a deep breath and concentrated on gathering the energy around her until her fingertips sparked with it. She carefully placed her hand on the control board and felt her way around the flow of the circuitry, creating a mental map of the rocket by the flow of energy through and around it, and doing her best to ignore that bright red glow of human generated electricity permeating the hull in one spot.

Where was it? Where was it? Ah, there. She sent a trickle of energy through the circuit, and then a surge at just the right point, and *Pop!* She moved her hand over, keeping her eyes closed. Next, guidance. She gritted her teeth as the moans and groans grew louder. They were not going to be quiet out there, she could tell. Come on guys! She wanted to yell. Do you really want to bring all the guards running?

She focused her energy again and after a moment, the guidance system code scrolled past her eyelids like a computer screen. There. Easy. One little tweak was all it would take, and… Done.

And not a moment too soon either. The rocket shook faster and faster and Celestine's noises rose to a breathy squeak that Meilin thought was a sure sign that she was a screamer.

Meilin pondered her options. If Celestine brought the other guards down on them, she'd be stuck inside the rocket for who knew how long. There was no way she would be able to get out of it without being noticed. She made a decision.

Meilin let go of the strap. The door dropped open and down with a heavy *thunk* and she heard a muffled shriek. She flicked her camera open on her com as she climbed out of the rocket. She clicked a few frames of the couple's surprised faces. His pants were around his ankles and her dress was rucked up in a big pink floofy cloud around them, her legs wrapped around his waist. But hey, who was Meilin to judge? She pulled the door screws out of her pocket, set them carefully on the ground and backed away.

"Hey you two, don't let me interrupt! Don't worry, Cel. I won't show these pics and audio to anyone. Not a soul I swear, just so long as you don't tell anyone I got curious and had to take a midnight peek inside the rocket. Deal?" They were frozen in shock. "I'm gonna take that as a yes from both of you. Have fun you crazy kids! Oh, and Guard, would you be a sweetheart and screw the door shut? When you're done?" She barely managed not to make a crack about any other screwing. Now *that* would be inappropriate.

"Thanks!" She winked at them and took off back to her room. In the hall, she managed to loudly waylay the guards heading their way on their rotation and direct them instead to the main floor Great Room. She was sure she'd heard a commotion there, she said, as she was out trying to walk off her terrible insomnia. She got back to her room and leaned against the closed door, taking a big breath. Mission accomplished.

Chapter 15:

MEILIN · IT WAS THE CLEANING DROID

The next day, Yun received word from the Rebels and sent Meilin back in to take more footage of the military compound. By now, all the princesses were going along to the daily trainings, except Celestine and Kaletra who said they were getting the perfect amount of exercise in their sleep, thanks to the newest in high-tech exer-sleep pods. And Yun had started bringing an equal number of maids, cooks, and seamstresses. Meilin was delighted.

And after the workout, she walked out amongst the crowd and snuck off to the armory. Looking at those rows upon rows of synthetic soldiers, her hands began to tingle. She could start taking these droids, and blasters out of the equation now, one by one shorting them out, but she held off. If she did and it was discovered, the Royals would know they had a rat in the palace, and they wanted to keep that secret as long as possible.

So, she merely took video and mentally shook her head at the ridiculous amount of access one blood test had given her. As soon as she was through, she headed back to her suite. She was in the underground hall between the military compound and the palace when she heard the Prince's voice and froze.

"No, you cannot film the dates from a closer vantage," he was saying to someone. "In fact, your vid crew needs to back off. And no, I will not grant pre- and post-date interviews about each of the girls. This whole thing is enough of a farce as it is."

"But, Your Highness, the Empress said—" a pushy woman's

voice replied, sounding like the Royal vid host that had been conducting interviews with the princesses all week, and announcing the play-by-play of the dates for the viewing public.

"I know what the Empress said," he cut her off. "That I was to go on dates with the princesses. I am allowing you to film them, from afar, because my mother thinks it makes for good public relations, but no more. Now if you'll excuse me."

And… he was coming her way. Not wanting him to think she was spying on him, Meilin ducked into a nearby cleaning droid closet, leaving the door cracked to continue eavesdropping.

"Oh, Your Highness, just one short interview before you go," the woman called, clearly not taking the hint. "It won't take but a minute." Then her sweet voice changed, dropping in volume as if she was talking into a com. "Get that vid crew here now," she ordered someone.

"No. No more interviews now, thank you," Prince Cor said and she saw him round the corner at a fast walk, looking pursued.

Meilin heard the vid host's voice still around the corner and didn't think. She quickly opened the door and pulled a surprised Prince Cor inside with a finger to her lips. She closed the door and held the door handle so it wouldn't turn.

"What are you—?" he whispered.

"Shh!" she hissed and they heard multiple pairs of footsteps round the corner of the hall outside.

"Now where did he go?" the vid host demanded. Someone tried the closet door, but Meilin held the handle firm.

"Locked," the woman said. "He can't be far. Come on!" she said and they heard running steps fade outside.

"Um, thanks," Prince Cor said. "Why did you help me?"

"I don't know." Meilin was asking herself the same question. "It just seemed like you needed it."

"Oh." He regarded her skeptically.

"And," she sighed. "I guess to say sorry for calling you useless the other day. Maybe that was overly harsh."

He gave a half laugh. "From you, I'll take that as a compliment. What are you doing in here anyway?"

"I was taking the long way back from the training room when I heard you talking in the hall with that vid host." She didn't have to feign a shudder. "I didn't want the vid crew to think I was eavesdropping on the Prince."

"Were you?"

"No!" Meilin crossed her arms and took a step back, bumping into a cleaning droid that beeped to life with a rainbow of lights across its front panel and started hovering forward, with a vacuum coming to life.

"Eep!" she jumped forward and spun, sending a side fist into its waist-high cranium. It crashed back into the shelves of cleaning supplies, causing an avalanche of cleaners and droid refills to come crashing down on them. And Meilin found herself in Prince Cor's arms as he protected her from the avalanche of supplies. The offending droid gave a sad burble and went dark.

Meilin clapped a hand over her mouth, but couldn't suppress the giggle that escaped. She looked up at the Prince to find him laughing too, and that he was alarmingly close, smooshed up against her in the mess.

"That was my favorite childhood droid," he said. "And you

killed her.”

“Uh, it attacked me first?”

“She,” he corrected, but there was a twinkle present in his eyes. A smile broke across his face. “Kidding. You should see the look on your face though.” He laughed and she realized they were so close, she could feel the vibration of his energy into hers. She shivered. His arms, still loosely around her tightened incrementally, but she found she didn’t mind that at all.

He let her go slowly and began picking up the mess, stacking it all back on the shelves.

“You know, I’ve always hated the vid crews,” he said after a moment. “I used to lay around all day when they were filming, trying to be as boring as possible in protest, but it didn’t work. Now I tend to stay in the military complex as much as possible, where they’re not allowed for security reasons.”

Meilin felt a twinge of guilt about the tiny camera atop her head. She hoped she’d remembered to turn it off.

“So, I usually only have to endure them when I’m in the palace, but lately with this ridiculous princess competition, it seems like I’m dealing with them all the time.”

“So, you didn’t want to choose a bride?”

He looked up at her wryly from his stooped position and righted the droid back into the corner. “No, this is not how I would’ve chosen to find anyone.”

“Why are you going along with it then?”

“She is the Empress.”

“Yeah, but—”

The droid chose that moment to come back to life, beeping

and whirring erratically and seeming to come straight at Meilin.

"Ahh!" she shrieked and gave it a sharp front kick back into the shelves, making it rain rags and cleaners once more.

Cor grabbed her into his chest with a sigh, taking the brunt of the deluge on his broad shoulders. She looked up at him sheepishly.

"You really don't like droids, do you?" He laughed down at her.

"Hate them." She seemed drawn into his cocobenne eyes.

"Well, I don't think that one will bother you anymore." But neither of them looked at the now silent droid.

"Oh, your only childhood friend," she murmured. "I'm sure someone around here will fix it for you."

"Her," he murmured back with that twinkle in his eye again. "Well, if they can't, you know what that means."

"No, what?" she asked, but her eyes were focused on how his full lips moved when he spoke.

"That *you'll* just have to be my friend. Maybe even go on that date with me."

"Mmm," she mumbled, much more interested in those lips that were a hairs breadth away from hers.

And then the door jerked open. They jumped apart and threw their arms over their eyes as spot lights shone into the closet.

"There he is!" someone shouted. "And Princess Meilin, what a surprise! Did you two plan to meet in here? How romantic! But what was that racket we heard?" The vid show host was practically giddy as they threw up their arms to cover their eyes. Meilin pushed her way out of the closet and through the vid crew, only wanting to get away.

"Princess Meilin!" The Prince shouted after her, but she just put her head down and ran to lock herself in her suite.

hapter 16:

MEILIN - THE DATE

Why was she so embarrassed? She lay on her bed an hour later, her arm over her eyes. So she'd been caught in a closet with the Prince. They were both adults, single, and he was hot as chili oil, so what? Still *everyone* would see that vid and smirk at her the way Yun was now, while she reviewed the end of the footage from Meilin's hairpiece camera. She had not remembered to turn it off after the armory.

She knew trying to convince Yun to withhold the end of that vid from Commander Zhang was pointless, so she kept her mouth shut. What she needed to do was convince herself that she didn't care. The Rebels could see it; she was just acting her part. The princesses could see the vid show; honestly, could they blame her? It didn't mean she wanted to marry the guy.

She was glad though, that she'd already reprogrammed the rocket because getting past the paparazzi at her door would have been impossible now. As it was, the Empress refused Meilin's request to take her meals in her suite, so she had to make her way through the vid crew to dinner and endure the glares of at least half the girls, in addition to the measuring stare of the Empress. After all, Meilin was already technically a real princess. She didn't need to win the Prince to be allowed to stay.

Only Imogen and Orencia spared her any sympathy and tried to help deflect Kaletra's poison tongue. Celestine remained uncharacteristically silent, though her face could have frozen lava.

And the Prince was off on a date with another girl. Of course. His engagement ball was coming up in only a few days. He had to pick someone, the Empress had decreed it. Some part of her hoped he was miserable for not standing up to Mommy.

Another unmarked package arrived for Meilin that night. Yun accepted it through the media's yelled questions and filming through the partially open door. Meilin stayed out of sight until the door was closed.

The package held shoes this time, not fancy, high-heeled torture shoes, but outdoor walking shoes. She unfolded the note inside and examined his straight forward scrawl.

THE DROID DIDN'T MAKE IT.

TOMORROW, 6AM, SHUTTLE BAY. DITCH THE VID CREW WITH ME? WEAR FATIGUES AND THE WALKING SHOES. LEAVE THE LIFTED TORTURE DEVICES HERE. - COR

Again, she couldn't stop a smile from spreading across her face, even as Yun snatched the note from her. Yun let out a squeal before slapping her hand over her mouth and looking at the door. Her expression then changed from excitement to concern.

"You do know this mutual crush you two have going is doomed to end with a bang in a few days, right?" Yun said.

Meilin straightened out her expression. "I don't know what you're talking about."

"Meilin!" she hissed, looking toward the door as if the vid crew could hear through the heavy wood. "You know exactly what I'm talking about."

Yeah, she did. The bomb she had reprogrammed would send an electro-mag pulse through the Jewel's dome, allowing the Rebels in to dethrone the Empress, and by extension, the Prince.

"But Cor isn't his mother," she whispered back. "And he doesn't *act* like he's planning on attacking Lyric. That barbarian I saw—"

"Listen to yourself! Cor is it now?" Yun shook her head and continued in a whisper. "Look, you saw unverified video of a barbarian with an unusual weapon. That's all. It's not proof of anything, and Command isn't going to change the plan without proof. The Empress has done too much damage to stop now." She shook her head again. "I hope you enjoy your date with *Cor* tomorrow. I'll be sleeping in." She walked to the door, jerked it open and barged through the surprised paparazzi.

※ ※ ※

"Where are we going?" she asked the Prince when she slipped into the palace shuttle bay early the next morning, relieved to have found no media people at her door or along the way. She wore her fatigues, walking shoes, and a translator earpiece that had also been included in the package. But she had no idea what was going on.

"You'll see," he answered mysteriously and turned, not to a shiny Royal shuttle, but to a dirty, non-descript one. She was intrigued but didn't ask again. She'd expected him to take her on the Jewel's tram, around to one of the moon's domes like he had the other girls. Perhaps to the farm dome with the field and the baby goats. Or the dinner theater with the white linens and bejeweled table settings. Only Meilin and Imogen acknowledged that the

Royal event planner had arranged each outing. The others didn't care to remember that piece, and pointing it out to them had just seemed mean.

But this, she stepped aboard the dirty shuttle and looked around doubtfully, this did not fit the mold of a Royal date. He couldn't have found out why she was really there, could he?

"Look, I know I can be a pain in the rear sometimes, but you can't just jettison me out into space." She turned in the doorway and he threw his head back and laughed, then stepped close. She stood her ground, but he merely cupped her cheek and brushed it with his thumb.

"Wouldn't dream of it, Princess."

She felt herself blush despite herself and scooted back into the shuttle's small available space to take a seat.

"Don't call me that." She scowled.

"All right. Meilin," he said softly.

And she realized her mistake. Her name coming from his lips was more personal than "Princess." The back half of the shuttle was filled with boxes and crates stacked to the ceiling, with not one, but at least two dozen picnic hampers stacked in front. To her surprise and relief, there were no servants or vid crew on board.

While Prince Cor sat in the pilot's seat and started the engine to a well-tuned *thrum,* she peeked in the top-most hampers at the huge volume of food the kitchens had packed for them.

"This is enough food for an army! How much do you think I can eat, anyway?"

He laughed. "Well, judging from the beef on your first night here," he joked and she made a face at him. "Come sit up here if you like. The view's better," he said. "Unless you want to keep snooping."

"Keep snooping, thanks," she said. Moving the heavy hampers, she looked in the boxes. They were filled with more food. This time, cases of dried beans, noodles, canned vegetables and flubber butter. What was he up to? The long, black case on the bottom though, she'd be damned if that wasn't a weapons case. But she'd have to move all the ones on top to reach it.

After her curiosity was thoroughly peaked, she went up front to sit in the co-pilot's seat and squinted at him. "What are we doing?" He opened his mouth, but she cut him off. "I know, I know. Wait and see. Sheesh."

He grinned at her. "Is this the part where you warn me not to screw with you?"

"I have moves you haven't even seen yet."

"I have no doubt about that." He gave her a sexy eyebrow quirk and her insides squeeshed. Sheesh, calm down, libido. He surely gave every one of those other girls that same look. He's probably patented it. She gave him a look in return that said she wasn't impressed—and yawned.

He laughed again and she looked out the window, trying not to react to it. Ugh. What did it say about her that she had a secret pocket full of poisoned candies for his mother, and yet she was turned on by his sexy laugh? It had to be some sort of moon-induced psychosis.

They were now entering orbit around Gallaius and before long they were gliding through the atmosphere, much more smoothly than she would have thought possible.

"We're going to the surface?" she blurted.

He gave a nod and smoothly piloted them above the trees, looking for something.

"What are you—oh. Huh." She saw something that didn't quite blend in and after a minute of focusing on it, realized it was a circular encampment of camouflaged tents. If she hadn't been looking, she would have missed it.

They got closer and landed, several soldiers running out to greet Cor with salutes, and bows for her, and started to unload. Out the door, at the center of the encampment she could see people. Not soldiers, at least not most of them, but ordinary women and men working, and children playing.

"Civilians?" she turned to him incredulously. "Why do you have civilians down here on a radiated planet?"

"No, not civilians from the Jewel. Survivors."

"Survivors? I thought the only survivors were barbarians." Which these people obviously were not.

"So did we, until recently. There are pockets here and there of people who survived the nuclear winter underground before coming up to scavenge. They surface now to grow food; their supplies are depleted. Except…" he trailed off.

"They're hunted," Meilin realized, horrified. He nodded. "So, you're supplying and training them?" She remembered Cor and his schmoozy second in command convincing the Empress that it was her idea. Another nod.

The same man, with a Captain's insignia on his shoulder, came along with the soldiers to unload the shuttle. They offloaded the

boxes and crates directly into the arms of normal, everyday looking people who wore tattered and patched together remnants of
vintage Gallaian clothing. Unlike everyone on the Jewel above,
men and women both wore serviceable work wear. Meilin was
glad Cor had instructed her to wear her fatigues rather than a
fancy dress for their date.

Captain Orin, as he was introduced to her, bowed and handed
each of them a plastic wrapped package. Cor immediately threw
his into a box in the corner of the shuttle that held a large number
of the same multi-colored packages.

"Thank you, Orin," he said. "Should the Empress ask, I will
tell her you delivered the rad suits to us as ordered. You may, of
course, forget to inform her that I chose not to put mine on."

"Of course, my Prince," Orin drawled, with a smile between
friends.

"The princess can decide whether or not to wear hers."

"No one else seems to be wearing a radiation suit?" Meilin
observed.

"Our best scientists have shown numerous times, that radiation levels have returned to pre-annihilation levels. Because this
is twenty years earlier than Mother was told all her life to expect,
she insists that I wear a suit when on Gallaius. I'd appreciate it if
you didn't tell her otherwise."

She squinted at him, then tossed her package into the box as
well. He grinned and she felt the rush of a shared secret.

"Come. I know it's breakfast time for us, but it'll be lunch
here soon. Let me show you around first." They walked through
camp, passing soldiers who saluted Cor and civilians who bowed

and curtsied as they carried supplies to wherever they were needed. Cor seemed different here, at ease somehow.

"First aid tent, mess hall, bathroom and shower setup." He turned to her. "You know the nice thing about being on planet?" She shook her head, bemused and charmed by his enthusiasm. "You can just dig down and hit water, enough for all our needs. I suppose that's not so amazing to someone from Lyric."

They passed women and men preparing the food they'd brought on long outdoor tables. Meilin and Cor reached the edge of camp and he pointed to a low cave that opened into a hillside. Civilians in their colorful patches ducked in and out. Children played nearby, running amongst the soldiers' tents.

"They still live below ground?" she asked.

"It's all they know."

"But now that they've come back to the surface, the barbarians…"

"That's why we're here. They're still our people, even if Mother doesn't want to recognize that." He scowled.

"She doesn't want to protect them?"

He shook his head, a dark look on his face. "It doesn't follow what she was taught all her life. She doesn't want to admit they're anything but barbarians."

"And who are the barbarians, exactly?"

"Survivors, but they came to the surface too early. Most died from radiation poisoning because they didn't have enough supplies and equipment for many years underground. That takes a hell of a lot of pre-planning, and most people didn't do it. These people here prepared exhaustively beforehand. They have a water and reclamation system, hydroponic gardens, methane generators to run grow lamps, and exhaust systems. The barbarians had none of that, and they scraped and fought each other to survive while we did nothing above. Their first generations after the bombs largely died early, from horrible cancers and radiation poisoning. It's no wonder they're the way they are; they've known nothing but war."

"You sound like you feel sorry for them."

"Don't you?" he asked. "Their lives for at least three generations now have been short and brutal. But that doesn't mean I have the luxury of condoning what they're doing. We're here to protect the peaceful, and to find a solution for those who aren't."

"And the Empress…" Meilin trailed off.

"The Empress believed those before her who said there was nothing they could do. That the people down here weren't subjects, but unfortunate gruesome casualties to be ignored. Any survivors wouldn't survive long."

"So that was the official position, until they started interfering with the Empress's mining expeditions? And then you started recruiting soldiers from Lyric."

He raised a surprised eyebrow, but nodded. "Yes. You must have heard that our scientists created drones, but they haven't been entirely successful. Real soldiers are the only way right now."

She squinted at him. "Why?" But she thought she knew. That barbarian she'd seen on the Prince's com pad had been carrying a very non-barbarian EMP blaster that took out a shuttle. She didn't have to guess what it did to the drones.

He cleared his throat. "Uh, hey, would you like a tour of the underground before our picnic? I think I can swing that. Hang on a sec." He turned away, seeming embarrassed.

Cor did indeed get permission, because really, who was going to deny the Crown Prince? And the daughter of the Gallaian leader, Sying, met them at the cave entrance with a reserved smile. They entered and followed hidden stairs down and down and down. As they descended into darkness, a brilliant blue glow suffused their hostess, and the people all around them. Meilin tried not to gawk at the men, women, and children who walked by in crowded corridors, glowing blue. There was no need for artificial lighting down here.

Meilin turned to Cor, but he anticipated her question.

"It's known as Cherenkov radiation," he said, leaning in to whisper in her ear. She shivered at his closeness and tried to concentrate on his words instead. "They've absorbed so much radiation, for generations, that those who survived emit their own from within. It's a miracle of adaptation, really. We can only see it because the human body is mostly water."

"So, why couldn't we see it outside?"

"Not strong enough during the day. You can see it outside at night though. Another reason for them to live underground."

The tour included some small living quarters, a few hydroponic gardens lit by full-spectrum sun lamps, and some depleted storerooms, but Meilin got the feeling that the Gallaian underground was much bigger. She was about to ask what was down another set of stairs when their tour was cut short. Sying announced that she really must help with the unloading, it was her duty as the leader's daughter. Though Meilin would have been happy to explore on their own, Cor offered to help haul and stack supplies.

Meilin found herself alone with their glowing hostess a short while later, in a storeroom stocking the cases of noodles, black beans, and canned vegetables that Meilin and Cor had brought. By and large, these people were vegetarian, by necessity. Hunting irradiated animals was forbidden.

Wondering how large a population was here, she closed her eyes and felt outward with her Gift. She felt pockets of the Gallaians' radiation several stories below her location, and stretching outward as far as she could feel. She couldn't tell how many there were, a few hundred was her best guess. She stretched her Gift, following an especially bright path of radiation, several stories down, and traveling outward in what must have been a tunnel that faded out at the edge of her Gift. Some of the radiation sparks there were stronger, but she couldn't tell if that meant more people, or stronger radioactive energy from something else. But the feeling there was different from the rest of the underground. It felt, especially those brighter sparks, corrupted, and dirty. She'd never felt anything like it, though of course she'd never felt anything like these Gallaians either, and she wondered if Cor knew how extensive this underground compound was, and what was in that tunnel.

Meilin opened her eyes, and realized she'd let the silence stretch too long to be polite between herself and Sying as they stacked supplies. Cor and the others still hadn't come back with another load, and Meilin felt compelled to say something.

"Your glow is very pretty. Useful too," she offered.

The young woman turned and looked at her guardedly for a moment. "I'd gladly give it up for any one of my family back," she said finally.

Meilin swallowed. These people, in that way, they were the same as Lyrans. She looked around, but they were still alone.

"I feel the same way," she said. She held out her hand, palm up and brought forth a white-hot ball of energy, so bright it was blinding, and extinguished it just as fast when the girl gasped and stepped back.

"The plague." Sying held her hands up in front of herself.

"You know about it?" Meilin asked and immediately reassured her, "I'm not a carrier. Do you think the Prince would be with me, would have brought me here if I was?"

Sying looked back at Meilin in consideration. "No," she said slowly. "I expect he'd be dead." Meilin nodded. "Like your people on Lyric."

"And my family, yes."

"We heard there was a cure. They didn't get it in time?" she asked. Meilin shook her head. "And neither did you." She reached out cautiously and took Meilin's hand, turning it palm up again. Meilin created another ball of energy, this time, pea-sized, perched on her finger. "But you survived." Meilin nodded.

The girl looked into her face. "Does he know?" she asked. Meilin paused, then crushed the flame between her fingers. Sharing this had been stupid. She wondered what the girl would do with the information.

But Sying surprised Meilin, taking her by the shoulders looking her in the eye. "I see you, sister," she said in the old tongue.

The device in Meilin's ear translated a beat later and tears sprang to her eyes. The girl smiled, not happily, but the hard smile of a survivor, and hugged her. Meilin was stiff at first, but then relaxed. She whispered the old words back to her, just before they heard the men on the stairs.

And then Cor stood silently in the doorway, a look of curiosity on his face as the two young women separated. He moved past them to stack his cases of food with the others until they reached the ceiling.

"Ready for lunch?" he asked Meilin. She nodded and said good-bye to Sying, wanting to say more, but unable to find the words. They started up the people-lit stairs. Cor waited until they'd exited the underground into the sunlight. "What did you say to her?"

Meilin shrugged. "I just…" she couldn't tell him the truth, "…told her I was sorry for their many losses."

"That's it?" he asked.

"Yeah."

He grunted and picked up a picnic basket. She wasn't sure he believed her as he led the way away from the long outdoor meal service tables and their seemingly endless twin lines of people waiting for food, and down a deserted arched path of berry bushes. Meilin looked at him out of the corner of her eye. Overgrown bushes lined the path on either side, giving way to a groomed tunnel of vines that looked something like the grapes that had been brought from Earth centuries ago. Other paths crossed theirs and she saw that each one held a different kind of berry on its trellised arbors.

"It's a big garden?" Meilin asked.

"Yes, circular. We're going to the center. I want to show you what makes all of this possible." They kept walking and she counted at least ten paths crossing theirs. Berries gave way to fruit bushes and vegetable plots. At center she could see...

"A tree?" she asked skeptically.

He laughed. "A very special tree." It was huge and draped almost to the ground with long tendrils of green veined with purple. And the shadow under the tree actually seemed brighter than any shady spot should have been. She silently felt toward it with her Gift. It felt unthreatening, though it thrummed with energy and vitality. Glowing translucent fruits hung from the branches over a carpet of dark red beneath. She stared up at them while Cor ducked under the curtain of leafy tendrils and laid out a picnic on the thick, growing carpet of something like red clover.

"What kind of tree is this?" Meilin ducked too and walked around the tree trunk, beneath the canopy of draping leaves, looking up at the white fruit. She realized suddenly that she had seen it before, aboard the *Temerity*, when Governor Fong had given one as a present to her commander. In the shade, it glowed bright blue through the light skin, just like the Gallaian survivors. She reached up and picked one of the pear-like fruits, accidentally nicking the pale skin and finding that it bled bright blue from the flesh inside. Her eyes widened as she felt the juice pulse into her palm, sending a shiver up her spine.

"Oh," she said in surprise, staring at it. Her mouth began to water. Cor plucked it from her hand and quickly tossed it into a metal bin left nearby that shut with a reverberating *clang* with the fruit inside.

"Radioactive," he said. "The baskets are lead-lined. The locals carefully take the fruit before it falls and give it as a "peace offering" to the barbarians." She shook out her hand which tingled. He uncapped his water flask and grabbed her wrist, rinsing the juice off.

"Does it work?"

"As a peace offering?" He cocked an eyebrow at her. "No." He smirked. She watched the contaminated water fall on the red clover at their feet, and it shivered, the red leaves brightening for a moment before returning to normal.

"So, the barbarians don't figure out the fruit is making them sick?"

"It's euphoric, a drug. The barbarians started out sick. They don't care that the fruit is making them worse." He unpacked and spread out their lunch, separating a bamboo steamer filled with dim sum. "We've been testing this tree, the fruit, and the surrounding cropland for months. Turns out the tree absorbs radiation from the soil and groundwater, cleansing it, making it the perfect spot for crops. We don't know how the Gallaians figured it out, but it's helped keep them healthy. They've got these trees with their circular gardens growing all over this area, but this one is the oldest. It's genius really." He patted the soft clover beside the picnic for her to sit and she sank to her knees. "And the locals use the shady spots under the trees for a..." he hesitated as if carefully choosing the right word, "getaway from the cramped underground."

Meilin frowned, trying to figure out why he'd hesitated and

then realized what he meant. She felt herself blush, again dammit, and tried not to think about anything else local couples might do in the soft, curtained privacy under the trees. She looked up at the fruit still ripening and thought about the glowing blue flesh inside. "Are you sure the Gallaians don't eat those themselves?" she asked skeptically.

"No. I mean, yes. They already have enough radiation without ingesting more. They're very aware of that. And those that do try it and become hooked end up kicked out and joining the barbarians. Their name for it translates to 'evil fruit'. Evil fruit for evil people, they say. They're very strict about it."

Evil barbarians, and the Governor of Lyric? Somehow these fruits were ending up in Fong's hands. What did that mean?

"Did we get all the juice off?" he asked. Her concern must have shown on her face. "You're not feeling any effects, are you?" She shook her head, but he took her hand and rinsed it again, this time holding on to her hand, turning it over to inspect it under the glow of the fruit lights above. Electricity flowed between them that had nothing to do with the fruit. She swallowed and looked up at him, her breath catching in her throat.

She didn't understand how, or why, he did this to her. Every human body generated electricity, but with him she was more aware of the spark that jumped between them than with anyone she'd ever met. With him, she wanted to run her fingers along his skin and trace the arcs and currents. She looked into his handsome face with those dark brown eyes and time seemed to stand still.

He put his free hand down on the red moss behind her and

leaned back, his body now in close proximity to hers. She unconsciously wet her lips and watched his mouth part slightly. At the moment what she wanted, if she was honest with herself, was to find out what he tasted like.

"I guess we'd better eat, huh?" he asked gruffly in her ear, breaking the spell. She shivered and closed her eyes at the heat of his breath on her cheek before his words sank in. Food. He wanted to eat lunch. Right. Come on Meilin, get your act together.

This was such a bad idea, part of her realized in a far off, disconnected way. Yun had been right. He was the Prince and she was here to kill his mother and oust his government. But she was having trouble making herself pull away. She had few friends on the *Temerity*, and no one she was really close to, no one she felt this way with. It was like simply being close to Cor was intoxicating and invigorating all her senses at once. She hadn't been physically close to anyone in so long; she'd forgotten how nice it felt to be touched. Was that really so wrong?

He grasped a small, perfectly steamed dumpling with his chopsticks and brought it, dripping with sauce, to her lips. She took it, the flavors bursting together as she slowly chewed. He wiped a finger at a drop of sauce at the corner of her mouth and brought it to his own lips.

He grinned at her and she wanted to smack him. He was doing this on purpose.

Mustering as much princess-like dignity as she could, she selected a small, soft pork bun from a bamboo steamer and took a bite before offering it to him. Two could play this game. But again, he proved to be better at it. He held her hand in place and her eyes with his as he took slow bites of the sweet pork filling, his lips finally brushing her fingertips. She shivered, once again feeling the zing of electricity between them. She cleared her throat and looked around for something else to focus on, anything. She selected a sweet, juicy lychee from a bowl, eating it while he finished chewing, though he still refused to let go of her hand. She thought he was going to kiss her then, but instead he reached for a small pastry, sticky and covered in sesame seeds.

"Dessert already?" she asked, her voice husky before biting into the offered treat and its gooey, dark center. She took the other half from him and held it to his lips.

"Dessert always," he said, closing his lips around the sweet. He chewed for a moment, swallowing unhurriedly, before bringing her fingers to his lips and licking them clean, trapping her gaze with his the whole time. She found that she was holding her breath and biting her lip as his tongue caressed the tip of each finger.

"That's my job." He cupped her cheek in his hand and finally brought his mouth to hers, but he stopped a hair's breadth away and still didn't kiss her. Instead he reached out with his teeth and nibbled her lip, then soothed it with the tip of his tongue. The breath she had been holding came out in a soft moan.

She knew it was ridiculous. She was not a princess. None of this was real. But what felt real was his hand on her cheek, the heat of his body next to hers.

She came up to her knees and gripped the sides of his face in her hands, pressing her lips to his.

"Mmmm," he mumbled and kissed her back, pulling her

down to into his lap. "Impatient," he murmured.

"Mmmhmm," she agreed. He kissed his way down her neck, one arm wrapped around her back, pressing her close. He slowly unbuttoned the front of her military issue shirt with one hand, stopping three buttons down.

"Lace?" he asked, looking surprised, as his fingers brushed the trim of her silken undershirt.

She looked down at the lacy undergarment that had seemed so unnecessary a few weeks ago. "Well, you didn't exactly send me a sports bra to wear under the fatigues, did you?"

He looked down with relish on his face at the incongruity of lacy white silk under her military shirt. "Best oversight I ever had."

She moved over him again and he groaned, kissing her deeply while searching out the next button and encouraging her movements with his own. All she could think was that she wanted him, wanted to be with him, wanted to feel his skin against hers.

"Our lab needs more fruit, Highness," a muffled male voice said from somewhere in the circular garden paths. Meilin and Cor froze. *Shinse!* Was someone out there talking to the Prince? Meilin had the horrifying thought that someone would see them, that the vid crew from the Jewel had found them, again.

"Shh!" Another distant voice cut the speaker off sharply. "We don't talk of that with visitors around!" a slightly familiar female voice snapped, and the voices receded into the distance.

Meilin and Cor relaxed slightly, both of them out of breath.

Cor groaned, putting his arms around her and squeezing for a moment, resting his forehead against hers. "I guess this is not exactly the best spot for this," he said with a rueful chuckle and rebuttoned Meilin's shirt. She scooted back, both of them again occupying their own space. "I suppose we should pack up and get back before my guards come looking for us."

They packed up their mostly uneaten lunch and made their way back to the shuttle. The spell of their romantic picnic was broken and reality intruded.

Chapter 17:

MEILIN · ESCAPE BY CANDY

That voice, had that been… Sying? Meilin thought so, but was the man calling *her* Highness? That's what it had sounded like, but Meilin had no idea how the Gallaian leadership worked. Meilin pondered what they'd heard as she and Cor walked back to the shuttle. Someone had helpfully re-parked it under the natural cover of the nearby forest so they wouldn't have to walk through the encampment again. And possibly to give them some of the privacy they could have used earlier. Meilin wondered if Captain Orin had been the thoughtful one, or if it had been someone else.

"They're still very secretive about their underground with us, if you hadn't guessed," Cor said. "We know they must have extensive underground labs, for them to have survived the high levels of radiation they were exposed to and be as healthy as they are. We also know they have advanced water reclamation and sanitization systems, but they won't show us any farther down there than what you saw today." But Cor didn't seem overly frustrated by this lack of sharing. "You can understand though, why they'd be protective of the technologies that kept them alive."

She nodded. "Why did you show me all this?" she wondered aloud. And now that her brain was functioning again, she felt conflicted. How could Cor be helping *these* people so much, but not even care about what he and his mother were doing to *her* people, to Lyrans?

"I thought you could handle it. And I thought I could trust

you," Cor said and she had a ping of conscience. "Can I?"

Instead of answering, she asked, "Why are you keeping these survivors secret? Don't you think Lyric should know what all the supplies we send are going for? People there think you're amassing an army."

"I am."

She stared at him at that bald admission and hesitated. He couldn't be saying what that sounded like, could he? Some Lyrans blamed the Rebels, but most knew that one way or another, if the tithes weren't paid, an attack against them was coming. By all reports, Governor Fong's thug collections had gotten worse, but the people had no more to give. However… it didn't seem like Cor wanted to hurt Lyric. Or maybe she just didn't want to believe it?

"*Why* are you raising an army?" she asked quietly.

He frowned, as if confused by her question. "Well, the barbarians... I mean, you must realize we'll have to fight to get the planet back."

"But your mother and the Royals before her have made it clear that they don't *want* Gallaius back. That they consider it ruined." They reached the shuttle and she looked around at the beautiful, if young, forest around her. If the planet had been ruined, it obviously wasn't any longer.

"My mother grew up her whole life being told the planet wouldn't recover for centuries, but it is, faster than our best scientists knew. Probably in part because of the radiation absorbing trees. She'll come around." He opened the shuttle door, still frowning at her. "Why else would I raise an army?"

"Ugh!" Meilin threw up her hands and stomped aboard the shuttle. Was he really this dense?

"What?" He entered after her and shut the door. Though empty now, the space felt cramped compared to the forest and she wished she'd stayed outside.

"It's honestly never occurred to you that raising an army might be interpreted some other way by the people of Lyric?"

There was more confused staring. "Are you saying... people on Lyric think I'm going to attack *them?*" He was either a good actor, or he really hadn't thought of it. She wasn't sure which was worse.

"Yes!"

"Why?"

Meilin sealed her lips shut and turned around. He took hold of her shoulders and spun her back.

"Why would they think I want to attack Lyric, Meilin?"

"Because we can't pay your stupid tithes anymore! Your taxes keep going up and up. Add in the Governor's increasing percentage to cover collection and you're sucking us dry!"

He seemed speechless for once.

"Haven't you *noticed?* Fewer and fewer farms and businesses can pay the full amount. They're just getting farther and farther behind. So the Governor hires more "collectors" and charges us their fees."

"Meilin," he started slowly. "We haven't raised the tithe in years. The Governor is paid by the Crown. He's not authorized to add any fees or percentage. He's not supposed to hire thugs to collect for him."

"Are you saying you didn't *know?* How could you have not known?"

"No, I didn't know! What else is he doing? Is this why the Rebels hate us? Fong just says that they're criminals who refuse to work."

She shut her mouth, crossed her arms, and refused to say any more.

A *wham, wham, wham!* came at the shuttle's front window and they both jerked around. They'd been so distracted, they hadn't noticed a huge, black barbarian vehicle had pulled up out of nowhere, smoking great puffs of black soot nearby. The hairy, crazed looking barbarian who'd pounded on the shuttle window to get their attention grinned, a ghastly blue glow emanating from inside his mouth even though it was daylight. He had a large blaster device pointed at them that Meilin unfortunately recognized.

"Get down!" Cor yelled and tackled her to the floor. Everything went dark.

A while later, Meilin wasn't sure how long exactly, she sat wondering if Skole's mutilation was self-inflicted, or if he'd really been at the wrong end of that many knife fights. She recognized him now, from the footage she'd seen on Cor's com during her first day on the Jewel. If his scars were self-inflicted, she might suggest he get help next time from someone with one, or even two, working eyes. If he'd just been in that many fights and gotten lucky, he was severely in need of some knife-fighting pointers.

Either way, she could help him out, if only he'd let her out of this cage.

She'd awoken from her energy weapon induced nap to see Cor looking at her with relief from a second bamboo and rope cage next to her own. His sword, of course, had been taken. She had to wonder briefly why it was fashionable for the Prince to carry a sword, while princesses were supposed to wander around helpless. If she got out of this, that was so going to change.

Seven barbarians sat around a campfire that smelled like it had been started with crude oil. They were eating through the food in the picnic basket while arguing and pointing at the shuttle. She wasn't sure what they were saying, but if she had to guess, it was something like, "Why doesn't it work? Make it fly, Grog." To which Grog replied, "Well, maybe you shouldn't have fired that lightening gun at it, stupid."

But perhaps this was giving them too much credit. Her earpiece translator was certainly not working anymore and she took it out, dropping it with a disgusted look.

"Meilin," Cor whispered. "Are you all right?"

She nodded and winced at the throbbing in her skull. "What kind of weapon is that?" She nodded at the large blaster with the distinctive inverted silver nose cone hanging from Skole's shoulder.

It was Cor's turn to wince. "Directional EMP. You must've taken a direct hit somehow."

Though filthy, she could tell that at one point it had been white, and was distinctly imperial in design. She stared at Cor in disbelief.

He sighed. "Yeah, they got it from us, when they attacked some of my men who were testing it a few months back. Too bad he doesn't understand that he just fried the circuitry on the shuttle. We thought it would take out their vehicles, but apparently, there are no important electronics to take out. But it sure works on our shuttles, droids, drones, and blasters."

"So it doesn't stop them, it stops us." And, more specifically, her. She wondered when she started thinking of Cor's forces as being on her side.

He nodded in disgust. "If they have any working electronics, they'd be inside their base of operations over there." He gestured to a hill about five miles in the distance and she could just make out a large structure like a giant bird cage atop it. She grunted. Which explained why Cor had placed so many of his own forces near the Gallaians if they were located this close to a barbarian stronghold. That was unfortunate, and also might have been nice to know.

"That wire cage appears to have shielded their compound from the EMP effect of the nuclear strikes of the Great War, so it's possible that they have uncompromised Terran data in there that would be priceless. That's one reason we haven't attacked them with conventional explosives. And of course, after our ancestors destroyed Gallaius, it is forbidden to manufacture large scale weaponry anymore. So, we're at an impasse, protecting our workers and assets, but not attacking them."

A junior barbarian saw they were awake and alerted the others. Their leader, Skole, stomped over and started yelling at Cor and Meilin and gesturing at the shuttle.

"I think he wants us to fix it," Cor said to Meilin, having discarded his own earpiece as well, before turning to the barbarian. "We can't," he yelled back, shaking his head, and then pointed at the EMP gun slung over the man's massive shoulder and chest. "You fried it!"

While Cor and the lead barbarian continued to have their pantomimed argument, the young one took a long stick and poked her through the bars in her ribs. He grinned a nasty grin that said he enjoyed bringing pain to those smaller than himself.

Skole stepped away and took an old-style com unit out of his pocket and tapped it, bringing it up to his ear. Cor grunted at this proof of his theory that some technology had survived in the barbarian stronghold. Skole started arguing with whoever was on the other end and gesturing at the shuttle. Meanwhile, Meilin kept an eye on the young barbarian and his pointed stick.

She pretended to look away and grabbed the stick on his next jab. She yanked on it so that his face smashed into the bars. He yanked it back and started yelling and waving it around with one hand while holding his bleeding nose with the other.

Skole yelled something at him, something Meilin took as, "Shut up! I'm on the com!" and a mid-level barbarian came and grabbed the stick from the young one. The mid-level barbarian then shook his finger at Meilin, before drawing it across his neck in a universal pantomime.

"I think he's saying—" Cor began.

"I can tell what he's saying, thanks," she said.

The young barbarian glared at her and went looking for another weapon, and Meilin had had enough. She made a show of looking through the pockets of her cargo pants and pulled out the small bag of poisoned sweets she'd been carrying since her arrival for the Empress. She pretended to fumble them, out through the cage bars, and they landed in the dirt.

"Oh no," she moaned loudly in despair. She reached through the bars for them, keeping an eye on the barbarians, especially the young one who'd just found Cor's sword, and pretended she couldn't quite reach the bag. The young barbarian scuttled forward, brandishing the sword at her and snatching the candies out from under her fingertips.

"Hey! Give those back!" she yelled, getting everyone's attention. "Those are special! For the Empress! You can't have them." She reached for the candies through the bars, waving her arm around. He just stepped back, grinning. He put the sword down and opened the tie of the little silken baggie.

"For Empress," he garbled.

"Yes, now give them back." She snapped her fingers imperiously at him. Meanwhile, from the corner of her eye, she saw that Skole was no longer arguing on his com, but listening, and his body language had gone from confrontational to subservient. Hmm.

The young barbarian took out one candy, unwrapped and sniffed it, but others came over to see, and the mid-level barbarian snatched it from his hand. A scuffle ensued, better than she could have hoped, the wrapped candies flying everywhere, and soon each barbarian was stuffing the golden sweets in his mouth, while scrambling for more. And then, one by one, they started dropping like flies.

Skole however, had only just finished talking with whoever it was on his com device and had missed the bait entirely. He watched the effects of the candies before wheeling around to bring the directed energy weapon up to bear on Meilin. She could see his finger tightening on the trigger, but she was already throwing her own bolt of energy from her fingertips straight into the cone of the weapon. It exploded in a flash of sparks and he tossed it up in scorched surprise before running for his filthy beast of a vehicle, and taking off.

Meilin ignored Cor's look of absolute shock, reached through the bars and picked up Cor's sword outside her cage, and began sawing at the ropes holding the cage shut. All was quiet, including Cor while she worked. He reached through his cage bars and picked up one of the worn wrappers from the dusty ground and sniffed it.

Chapter 18:

MEILIN - THE TRUTH COMES OUT

She opened her own cage and began sawing through the rope holding his cage shut, watching him warily. She'd just revealed everything to him. Now he knew that she was a plague survivor—which, since that hadn't shown on her Royal blood test, meant she had taken suppressors only attainable through the black market. Now he had to know where she had acquired her fighting skills—the Rebels. And now he knew too, that she'd been plotting to assassinate the Empress. The question was, what would he do?

She swung his door open and he stepped out calmly, looking around at the strewn bodies of the barbarians, still glowing blue out their limp and open mouths.

His hand was a striking cobra that knocked his sword away and wrapped its jaws around her upper arm, even as she tried to pull away.

"What is this, Meilin?" he snarled, holding up the worn golden wrapper. It was distinctive, with her family's crest stamped on each square. "The farm where these were made *burned down* six years ago! Where did you get these?"

For a moment, the acrid stench of burning mulberry trees filled her nostrils once more. The day she had buried her parents was the day her Gift had manifested in the burning destruction of everything they had.

She lifted her chin. "Who do you think burned it down?"

She issued a shock through her body, into his hand, forcing

him to let go. She rubbed her bicep where he'd squeezed and he backed away staring at her in horror. She felt the old anger surface and erupt through her skin with little sparks of electricity all over her body.

"That was *my* family's farm. We produced your mother's precious silk and golden candies. And when we all got the plague and couldn't pay our full tithe, your mother ordered that only her *loyal paying* subjects get the cure. I was seventeen. I worked day and night to make enough to settle our tithe, and when collection day arrived, they came and took everything. They beat me and my sick parents to come up with more, but it still wasn't enough to pay their *fees*. That was the day I vowed to learn to fight. So no one could do that to me or those I loved ever again.

"My parents *died* from your mother's cruelty, the Crown took the farm, and I got this *Gift*. Well, you can have it back."

She rotated her hand around and a ball of energy formed in it. She saw his eyes widen in alarm and she almost threw it, almost. But she wasn't seventeen anymore, and she controlled her Gift now. She let it dissipate.

"But before I burned the golden mulberry trees that kept her precious silk worms alive, I made one last batch of candy for our Empress. I have waited years to deliver them."

She watched his face harden as he put the rest of the pieces together. "There's only one thing wrong with your story, *Meilin,* if that's even your name. We mass produced that cure and sent enough for every person on Lyric. The order was that it would go to anyone who was sick."

"Don't lie. I may have been just a kid, but I heard Governor

Fong issue the edict from the Crown with my own ears."

"*Fong?* Fong withheld life-saving medicine saying it was the Crown's order? Why would he do that? Why have I never heard this before?"

"Because he's *your* appointee! He controls everything on Lyric. Why would we question that he was delivering and enforcing the Empress's will?"

Prince Cor squeezed his eyes shut and took a deep breath through flared nostrils. "Because as abrasive as my mother may be at times, she's not a monster," he said. He opened his mouth to say more, but was cut off by the arrival of his forces, ready for a battle that was already over.

"Your Majesty?" Captain Orin looked from Meilin to the Prince and back, clearly uncertain about what to do.

"Arrest her," said Cormorin. "She's not a princess, she's a Rebel spy sent to kill the Empress."

Chapter 19:

CORMORIN - GOVERNOR FONG ARRIVES

Stupid, Cor berated himself. He had to stop thinking about her. She'd plotted to kill the Empress, end of story. And still he was being stupidly merciful, sending her to the dungeon, and then the work camps on Lyric with the next transport. He shook his head as if to shake her out of it. Her smile, her snark, her laughter in brief, unguarded moments. He'd been duped.

But, that didn't *feel* right, somehow, some little part of him kept whispering. He'd had a long night of thinking over everything she'd said, all the whys and what ifs. So what if she hadn't actually given his mother the poisoned candies? That's what she was planning to do, right? Eventually. *But she hadn't done it. Why?*

Words of condemnation mixed in his brain with the urge to defend her, blending into a confusing stew of emotions. He'd looked back when she was taken away the day before. She had not, walking away with her head high, and her hands synth-cuffed behind her back.

It was now the morning of the engagement ball and he was dressed in an elaborate military dress uniform, and miserable. His mother would be expecting his choice at the ball that afternoon, but his only choice now sat in the dungeon. How could he have so thoroughly misread Meilin?

His mother had called him to the Great Room to welcome their first guests, and he was sitting there brooding when Governor Fong arrived from Lyric. He was presumably there for the engagement announcement, hoping, no expecting, that Cor would name his putrid daughter. The rotund, ruddy faced man was overdressed, if that was possible, in a shiny suit with jewels on his fingers, and with an overly large entourage… except, some of those definitely weren't the entourage type.

Cor looked more closely. Those had to be Rebels he realized, a dozen of them in cuffs and with hoods over their bent heads, looking defeated, and surrounded by thuggish looking guards, each with a newly shaven head and eyebrows. His mother straightened in interest on her throne, and Cor stood up, with his hand on his sword hilt.

The Governor bowed low to the Empress and kissed her hand when she graciously beckoned him forward.

"My Empress, you are looking radiant as usual," he schmoozed.

"Fong, what is all this?" she said, waving her hand imperiously from her throne.

"Rebels, Empress. I caught them on Lyric, plotting against the Crown. I brought them as a present in your honor, that our Prince and his team might interrogate them properly."

Cor scanned the chained prisoners. So, these were Meilin's Rebels. Their heads were covered so he couldn't see their faces, and they kept their heads down, silent. Cowed, or waiting?

His mother clapped her hands. "Take them to the dungeon!" The guards came forward and took the Rebels away. They were strangely docile, and their bound hands seemed less bruised and bloodied than he would have expected after fighting for their freedom and losing.

"You shall be handsomely rewarded, Governor Fong," his mother said.

But Fong demurred. "Loyalty to the Crown is its own reward, Your Majesty. My only hope is that after this day, we shall be closer than ever."

"Hmmm," his mother considered Fong and stood. She held out her arm to him and Cor tensed, wanting to stop her, to warn her away from the slimy Fong. But they had Royal guards nearby. She was perfectly safe. Fong jumped to eagerly accept the Empress's proffered arm.

"Let us walk, shall we? Cor?" She turned her head to him. "Walk with us. We must discuss the strengthening of our alliance with Governor Fong. You can let our new guests get settled in the dungeon before you welcome them."

Cor wanted to argue, but he couldn't help but be struck by the radiance of Fong's smile... or was that a faint blue glow from the depths of his mouth?

"Yes, Mother." And he took his mother's arm on her other side.

"Governor," she said. "Your daughter has been such a joy to have with us these past weeks. Don't you agree Cormorin?"

Cor gritted his teeth and smiled. Governor Fong smiled back.

Chapter 20:

MEILIN - OLD FRIENDS

The Prince hadn't spoken two words to her on the way back. He and a crew full of guards had flown with her back to the Jewel, all keeping their distance from her cuffed hands, and keeping her away from Prince Cor. When they'd landed, Cor had walked off without a word, his mask of indifference firmly in place. And the guards had escorted her to the palace dungeon.

She looked around at the stark whiteness of the simple, large holding cell. The walls, the floor, everything was made of some hard, white substance, the furniture seamlessly attached and made of the same stuff as if it had been grown in place. The only thing that wasn't the newest, most advanced in genteel prison technology was the lock on the door, which was an old-fashioned metal bolt and padlock, hastily located and installed before she got there. She could make the lights flicker, and she'd shorted out the audio-visual feeds keeping tabs on the cell, but otherwise she hadn't been able to do anything with her Gift. She felt absolutely alone, cold, and cut off from the world. She'd curled into herself and had a long night alone with thoughts of her failure.

She'd heard Captain Orin advise Cor not to speak with her again. He'd said that he would take care of sending her to one of the Lyran work camps. As Cor had walked away, she'd been tempted to call after him, but instead had turned her back. This was why she didn't do love, or even lust. Letting her guard down for someone had made her stupid. And look where that had gotten her.

It must have been morning. Someone delivered her a tray of food, the guard shift changed, and a while later, Meilin watched as at least a dozen hooded prisoners were shoved into the large holding cell with her. They kept their heads down as the guards removed their hoods, left the cell, and pressed the electronic release on their cuffs once the door was shut. Only when the guards had gone did the new prisoners grin to one another, and by then, Meilin had recognized the mid-grade members of the *Temerity's* Rebel crew, including her old drill sergeant, Xiaobo.

"It worked! We're in!" they whispered excitedly. And then they spotted Meilin.

"What are you doing in here, Wei?" Sumai, one of her not-quite-friends, not-quite-enemies asked in surprise.

"Caught." She shrugged as if it were no big deal. "They really caught all of you?"

"Yes. We're extremely upset!" said Li, an affable young officer whose kindness had stood out on the *Temerity*. His dark, hooded eyes, however told a different story and he practically vibrated with energy.

"Yeah, that sounds realistic." Meilin rolled her eyes.

The young man made an almost inaudible *shhh* and lifted his eyes to scan the ceiling and walls. Meilin had a hunch who they were working with in this coup.

Meilin shook her head. "I fried the cameras—don't worry about it. You're working with Fong, aren't you?"

He hesitated and then nodded. "Yes. He smuggled us in." He lowered his voice even more. "We'll be attacking during the engagement party."

"Fong is a liar," Meilin said. "You can't trust him."

The three of them were the most senior team leaders present, and they quickly gathered around Meilin. She was usually on decent terms with at least two of the three, but now they glared at her.

"Stop screwing with us," Xiaobo said. "Fong's the one that got us in here. The Commander turned this operation over to him."

"*Over* to him? I thought we were installing Commander Zhang as Empress. Not Fong!" Her voice went up and the others made quieting gestures.

"Shhh!"

"He's a snake," Meilin continued, though she lowered her voice. "It wasn't the Royals who limited the plague cure to only those who'd paid their tithe in full. That was Fong. *He* killed my family and probably some of yours too, for money, and land. I've been blaming the Royals all this time, but it was *Fong!*" The lights flickered in her agitation.

"Where'd you get that, Wei? The handsome prince? Did you fall for him after all?" Sumai sneered. "You've been all over the Royal News, you know."

"Thought we could at least count on you of anyone to not be brainwashed by the Royals and their fancy palace," Xiaobo said.

"All right everyone, calm down. Fong's just the public headpiece for this coup," Li told Meilin. "We needed someone the people will accept. But make no mistake, we're in charge. And we're the ones getting rewarded with all that confiscated farmland on Lyric. Think of it, Wei! No more hiding. Once we're in power, we get to go home, as citizens not outlaws."

"You think he'll wipe the slate clean for us?" Meilin asked incredulously. "He's going to throw us to the wolesqnas! Look where you are!"

"Look where *you* are. We're following the plan," Xiaobo said. "You're the one who screwed up and got thrown in here for real. Fong's coming with disguises to get us out. We've got to go disable the Jewel's droid army, seeing as they're likely protected from your EMP rocket. Then we take over. We were supposed to get you to come with us, if possible, to show us through the military compound, but now..." He shook his head in disgust at her failure in getting caught. "At least you reported that you completed your mission, before you turned on us. Correct?"

Meilin felt her eyes widen and she nodded woodenly. The rocket bomb. How could she have forgotten?

He grunted in satisfaction. "Now you just sit and let us do the rest, and you'll still be rewarded. But cross us and you'll see the inside of a work camp for the rest of your short, bitter life."

Meilin pretended to meekly sit and wait, all the while trying to figure out a way out of this cell. She had to turn that EMP rocket back into nothing more than pretty space fireworks.

Chapter 21:

MEILIN - THE PRINCE QUESTIONS THE GOVERNOR

Hours later, Meilin was still trying to think of a way to believably call the guard over to the cell door, with the key, when she heard a young woman's sweet voice briefly down the hall. A *thump* followed, along with a brief, surprised yelp, and another *thump*. Then the electronic locks *thunked* open and Yun was at the cell door, dressed in her maid's uniform. She unlocked the mechanical pad lock and swung the cell door open, surprising them all by stepping inside with a bag over her shoulder and her makeup case, and swinging the cell door shut again.

"It's cool," she interrupted their protests, "I've still got the keys." She showed them an old-fashioned metal key, and a small remote device. Xiaobo gestured to two of the Rebels to man the cell door and Yun turned to Meilin. "I didn't know the Commander turned over the Emperorship to Fong, I swear. He hurt my family too." She turned to the lead Rebels. "It's become clear to me, watching Meilin and Prince Cor, listening while they were on planet—"

Meilin gasped and put her hand to her head. The surveillance cam was still attached to her hairpiece. "But I turned that off," she exclaimed in horror.

"Yeah, and I turned it back on," Yun replied. Meilin winced in embarrassment. "I wasn't spying on you," Yun told her, "but I had a job to do. Anyway, back to what I was saying. It's become clear to me that Prince Cor is actually a good person. And Fong is not.

"But I'm still here to do my job for the Rebels. Fong was supposed to release you and give you disguises to get to the armory, correct? So you can disable that metal army before our invasion. But he hasn't come, has he?" Though he hesitated, Xiaobo shook his head.

"I don't know what Fong's game is, but I saw him escorted to his rooms hours ago. I don't think we can trust him to do his part. Here." Yun threw a bag to Li. He opened it to reveal three sets of fatigues. Yun set down her cosmetics case on a white bench and opened it. "Glad to see you've already got your heads shaved. Now let's get rid of those eyebrows and you can get out of here, as soldiers."

"At least someone's still doing their job," Xiaobo grunted, once he, Li, and Sumai were outfitted. "The rest of you, guard her." Xiaobo pointed at Meilin, and the three of them took the dungeon guards' weapons and snuck out.

Meilin turned to Yun and the rest of the Rebels. "You heard what's happening." She rotated her hand around the ball of energy that she had called into it. Except Yun, they all took a step back. "I'm getting out of here now to stop Fong. Don't make me electrocute you, because I will."

"Wait," Yun said and Meilin prepared to argue, but Yun merely held up her straight razor. "It's surprising how much eyebrows change your appearance. You need to be a soldier too now."

A short while later, Meilin and Yun knelt behind a large potted fern on the balcony above the Great Room. They'd used the excitement and confusion of the arriving guests as cover for a soldier and a maid to walk into the palace. Meilin was glad she wasn't alone, and Yun was the only one she would've trusted enough to come with her. The rest of the Rebels had grumbled, but hadn't followed. They were blindly waiting for Fong and the next stage of their plan.

Above the Great Room, the rocket still hung on display, like a giant, explosive chandelier. Cor and the Empress sat atop their thrones below, and Governor Fong was in front of them. The other guests were being shown to their rooms to freshen up before the party. Meilin peered down at her enemy, Fong, and itched to try her best impersonation of ancient Zeus on high, but Yun counseled her to be patient.

Meilin looked at the rope extending from the corner of the balcony rail up to the ceiling to suspend the shining rocket. She'd stolen a pocket knife from Yun's trussed up guards in lieu of a screw driver for the rocket's door, but now she was having serious doubts. Could she really climb the rope, dangle above the Prince, Empress, Fong, and a whole unit of guards below, work the screws one handed with a pocket knife, and slip into the rocket unnoticed? Yeah, and barbarians could fly. She was wondering where and when they would move the rocket for launch when she heard Cor speaking below.

She looked down to see Cor looking angry, and she thought for a moment he'd spotted her, but the Empress merely looked perplexed, patting his arm on the throne next to her.

"Governor Fong," Cor's voice rang out. "Did you six years ago, or at any time, withhold the plague medicine we sent to Lyric from families who could not pay their tithe to the Crown in full?"

Fong looked uncertain. "Well, my Prince, it was a difficult time and an excellent bargaining chip to get people to pay what they rightfully owed the Crown."

To Meilin's anger, the Empress nodded thoughtfully at this reasoning.

"But Governor," Cor tried again, "could you not see that withholding vital medicine would cause more infection and death of our people?" Meilin felt her frozen heart melt just a little for him.

Fong raised his hands, as if trying to slow this tide of anger. "But, my Prince, most of them did pay. And besides, I am certain that waiting until they paid did not extend the spread of the disease."

"Oh, you think not? And what of the reports that you increased our set tithe to the colonists to pay for your collection efforts?"

"My Lord, I was authorized by the Empress herself," he gave her a slimy little bow, "to hire agents as needed to collect her tithe."

"Did she authorize you to hire thugs to terrorize our people and increase her tithe to pay them?"

"Perhaps my agents were... overzealous a time or two," Fong conceded.

"Overzealous?" Cor asked with a haughty arch of his perfect black eyebrows. "They beat a young girl and her sick parents when they could not make your inflated tithe. They died without the cure. And that was the end of a silk farm that was highly valuable to the Empress and the Crown."

Even as Meilin recognized her own story, behind her Yun sighed, "He's in love with you, too." Her eyes shone with romance, but Meilin shook her head.

"He left me in the dungeons."

Below, Fong looked aghast. "My dear Prince, from where are you getting this information? I assure you, if anything like what you describe had happened, I would have reprimanded my agents myself, most severely."

Cor glared. "I notice you didn't answer my question, Fong. Did you increase the Crown's tithe to pay for your 'agents', or for any other purpose?"

"I did add a small amount for our trouble with collections—"

"How small?" The Empress now squinted at him.

"Merely five or ten percent, my Empress," he simpered. "I had to pay for—"

"Wasn't it twenty?" Cor cut in. "And who authorized you to increase the tithe at all? You are, after all, paid handsomely by the Crown for the purpose of performing collections." The Empress was now looking at Fong with clear eyes for what may have been the first time.

"It is a large territory. I was authorized to hire agents to collect as necessary—" Fong sputtered.

"At your own expense. Not to add any amount you chose to the Crown's tithe!" Cor turned to his mother. "Don't you see? This man has *caused* the Rebellion, claiming his actions are the Crown's!"

"Now see here—" Fong looked indignant.

"I can see Governor Fong, that I allowed you too much leeway, too much authority," the Empress said coldly. "I am disappointed."

Fong looked down as if cowed. "I am sorry, Empress. I assure you it won't happen again."

"See that it doesn't." The Empress took a small blue candy absently from her pocket and popped it in her mouth. She seemed to relax and her eyes glazed over a bit, giving her a softer focus. She waved her hand like she was waving away a fly. "We will deal with this later."

"What? Mother!" Cor exclaimed as Fong walked from the room, hiding his smirk until he was at the door.

"Now is not the time. Our guests are arriving. We have a celebration to put on, and you my son must go get ready to make your announcement."

"Mother, in light of everything, is now really the time—"

"Yes, my boy. You are not getting out of it," his mother said with a teasing wag of her golden painted fingertip and a lilt in her voice. "Get over your nerves. Today is the day you declare your princess and we shall not let anything ruin your happiest of days. Now go. Greet your guests and welcome them in." She pulled out another blue candy and unwrapped it, smoothing her elaborate skirts while waving him out the Great Room door.

And Meilin felt her heart break a little more as she watched Cor, so handsome in his finery, obediently leave to greet the guests for his engagement party. She felt her lip curl and turned to Yun, *"Where* exactly is his backbone?"

Yun shook her head.

Chapter 22:

CORMORIN - THE ENGAGEMENT PARTY

Cor left the Great Room and immediately pinged Orin on his com. "Where did Fong go?" he asked without preamble. "Please say you are having him followed."

"Of course. I am doing so myself now," Captain Orin whispered. "He is currently walking toward the transport bay. All guests have already arrived. There are no transports scheduled until tomorrow."

"What is he up to? Did he forget something aboard his shuttle?" Cor wondered aloud and took off in the direction of the transport bay, nodding to opulently dressed guests as he passed, but bypassing their attempts to get him to stop to talk. He didn't care what his mother wanted. He ground his teeth together and sped up. How could she not see it? Fong was corrupt, a criminal, and allowing him to remain in charge of Lyric was a huge mistake. Cor would do whatever it took to prove it. If anyone belonged in the dungeon, it was the Governor.

"Your guess is as good as mine, sir. Also, Your Majesty, the dungeon guards failed to report in a few minutes ago. I have sent a team to find out why. The last report said something strange; that the Rebels had shaved heads. I didn't think that was a custom on Lyric."

"No, nor I," Cor said. "Considerate of them." Cor considered the possible implications of that and almost changed course to the dungeons. But first, he needed to see what Fong was up to.

"Report immediately when you hear from your team. And, merely keep an eye on Fong and wait for me. I'm on my way."

When Cor got to the transport bay he nodded to Orin, who waited outside. The area appeared entirely empty of other people, even the guests' pilots had been invited into the palace for the engagement celebration. However, someone had left the shuttle bay lights on, and the bay door windows gave a straight view out to the lantern-lit palace lawn, with its launch tube for Fong's now suspicious fireworks rocket present. Cor was going to have to rethink that, after dealing with Fong.

Captain Orin pointed through the open door at the fanciest transport in the bay and whispered, "Governor Fong went toward his ship." Cor slid into the shuttle bay and behind the nearest transport. The governor's shiny, top of the line shuttle was nearby, and someone could be seen moving inside. Cor snuck around up to the shuttle's open, far side door and leaned nonchalantly against the side of the ship, watching. Fong had removed one of the floor panels and was kneeling over it with his rear in the air, reaching into the hidden space. He brought out a medium sized case, set it carefully on the floor, and replaced the floorboard. He picked up the case, turned around and shrieked at the sight of Cor.

"Governor Fong, you do know we have footmen to help with your luggage?" Cor said.

"My Prince, you startled me!" Fong held his hand to his barrel chest.

"What's in the case?" Cor growled.

"Well, I," Fong sniffed as if affronted. "A surprise gift for the

Empress, if you must know. Of course, you may see for yourself, my Prince, if you would like." He set the plain, black case down on the shuttle floor and flipped up the clasp. He began to raise the lid and Cor caught the barest glimpse of metal inside and reacted. With one hand, he slammed the case shut, into Fong's hands, and with the other, he snapped his fist into Fong's nose, hearing it crunch. Fong cried out and fell backward into the shuttle, holding his hands cupped over his nose.

Cor opened the case and spun it around to see fine clothes inside, at least one suit and a dress. *Shinse*, if he was wrong… He rummaged through the clothing, and found the flash of silver mostly buried at the bottom. He pulled out a blaster, with an inverted silver nose-cone.

"Where did you *get* this?" he demanded. The prototype had been stolen on Gallaius months ago, and Meilin had destroyed it the day before in the hands of a barbarian. Where had this clean, brand-new EMP blaster come from?

But instead of answering, the big man gave a yell, and dove out of the shuttle, grabbing at the weapon. They both hit the floor and Cor rolled back, using the big man's momentum to kick him up and over his head. He came up on top of Fong, with the blaster across his throat, pinning him to the ground.

"Prince Cor!" Orin yelled and ran toward them.

"Captain Orin, place this man under arrest. But first, I need to know exactly what he knows."

Chapter 28:

Yun and Meilin stared at each other.

"So, the Empress is an idiot and the Prince can't stand up to his mommy," Meilin said. "As soon as that rocket is launched and EMPs the dome, Commander Zhang and the rest of the Rebels from the *Temerity* will invade, but they've somehow been brainwashed into installing *Fong*. It's up to us. Fong can't be allowed to take over," said Meilin.

Yun grimaced. "But our cause… Deposing the Empress…"

"I don't know about you, but I signed up to stop Lyrans from dying. Right now, the Empress is exacting her tithe, true, but you heard Cor. All the misery being done in the name of the Crown is coming from Fong. I'm still not a fan of royalty, but if we allow Fong to gain power, everything will be ten times worse. We have to stop him."

Yun bit her lip and looked doubtful. "But, that could mean fighting our own people."

Meilin took a deep breath. "I know."

Yun gulped and then nodded.

"The best way I can see to avoid fighting the Rebels, and keep Fong out of power, is to keep the rest of the Rebels from invading and supporting Fong. I have to get aboard that rocket and change it back to fireworks." She looked up at the rocket hanging above and felt herself frown. "So they can celebrate the Prince," she muttered, "and whichever girl he chooses for his princess."

"He'd better not choose Celestine," Yun said darkly, exactly what Meilin was thinking, but that wasn't important now.

Meilin nodded and rubbed her hands together, checking that the Empress was otherwise occupied greeting her Royal guests as they entered the Great Room below. Her chances of not being seen weren't going to improve with waiting. Meilin stepped out of her hiding spot, reaching up to grab the rope on which the rocket hung. She climbed onto the balcony rail.

"Hide!" Yun hissed, yanking her back and behind a small grove of potted plants behind the balcony seats. Meilin watched in horror as a group of six splendidly dressed, hairless mole rat footmen arrived on their balcony. They untied the rocket from the wall, and waited. And waited. Meilin heard more and more activity below.

The footmen stood there in a line, all of them silently holding the rope, awaiting some signal. Finally, a fanfare of trumpets sounded below and they lowered the rocket carefully to the Great Room below.

From her spot behind the foliage, Meilin could only see the far edge of the Great Room below, which was now filling with opulently dressed guests, with a group of drummers and trumpeters off to one side. As soon as the rocket was safely down, the footmen on the balcony left and Meilin and Yun were alone again to watch through the railing. The footmen loaded the rocket onto a hover cart and with all the pomp and circumstance of a small parade, they opened the Great Room curtains to reveal large French doors, through which they pushed the rocket outside and across the lantern-lit patio. They crossed an impossibly green lawn under the dome, with beautiful, exorbitantly dressed guests trailing. And, when they reached the launch tube that lead to a closed door in the glass dome above, they carefully loaded the rocket inside.

"Oh, hallowed *shinse*, they're going to launch it!" Meilin exclaimed, her hands sparking on the wooden rail. Thankfully everyone below was focused outside.

"Shhh! No, no," Yun said soothingly. "They have to wait for the Prince to make his announcement. He's not even back yet. We've got time."

"Time? Seriously?" Meilin was not calming down. "How am I going to get aboard now? That thing is going to EMP the palace dome and it's my fault!"

"Well first, we've got to get you through that crowd unnoticed and unrecognized, and we need to hurry. Someone is going to notice soon that you're not in the dungeon. And right now, in that crowd, you are not going to blend in wearing that." She gestured to Meilin's fatigues.

"Oh really? I hadn't noticed." Meilin made a face at her.

"Wait here. I have an idea." And without waiting for a response, Yun flew off down the hall.

With no other choice, Meilin waited behind the balcony greenery, peering out at the Great Room below filling again with guests and servants carrying trays of mini pastries and assorted delicacies. An orchestra began playing classical music and guests continued to arrive in their finery. The Empress sat upon her throne, nibbling a moon cake, interspersed with sips of red Yangmei Jiu and another of those suspicious blue candies. Several of the princess candidates mingled nervously with the crowd, each in a different, amazingly fabulous dress in a rainbow of colors. It must have been some corruption of her personality due to her time here at the palace that Meilin felt envious and admiring of those gorgeous dresses.

The seamstress had measured Meilin for a gown as well, but she hadn't even gotten to see it finished, and she felt more than a twinge of disappointment. She pushed the feeling deep and told herself to buck up. She had more important things to worry about than moping about some silly dress. Like if Yun could find a way to get her to that rocket.

A few minutes later, Yun returned, a dress bag over one arm. "Put this on." She tossed Meilin the dress bag. "I swiped it from your room, it must have been delivered before you were arrested."

Meilin caught her breath when she unzipped the bag at the sight of the shimmering silk, imperial red with gold embroidery and a ridiculously large skirt and train. The fabric was old, produced by her family's farm in their heyday. It must have been saved for years for just this occasion. She felt her heart squeeze and adored it instantly, but tried not to let the moisture in her eyes show. Instead, she quickly stripped behind the potted trees and stepped into the impractical gown that felt like a silken cloud on her skin. Yun zipped her into it.

"The guards are looking for you," Yun said, "all over the palace and military base, but they're keeping it quiet, not wanting to alarm the guests. I don't think they expect to find you here, and they didn't even notice I was gone, so that's something at least."

Meilin nodded. The dress fit like a dream, but she was still too recognizable. Yun popped open her bag of tricks and dumped the whole thing out on the floor.

"What are you doing? We don't have time for a full makeup disguise."

Yun grunted agreement. "True. Plus, I arranged with Orencia, Imogen, and a few of the other girls for a distraction in a few minutes. They were so relieved you're all right, and they were completely on board when they learned you were trying to stop a coup." She pulled the bottom out of the makeup kit and pulled something out from underneath. A holo-hair emitter to replace the one she'd left in the dungeon, and if Meilin had to guess—

"A facial anti-rec veil, the best we have," Yun confirmed. She began to combine the hair emitter with the veil. "It's completely illegal of course, so don't get caught with it," she said, placing it on Meilin's scalp.

She felt nothing as the digital veil fell into place and became completely see-through, dark virtual hair straight to her shoulders and obscuring the sides of her face where the veil would be thinnest. She stood up, still behind the potted greenery. "How do I look?"

Yun smiled, half-dreamily, half gloating with success. "Like royalty. A princess candidate who no one will quite be able to place. It's perfect. Now go!" And Meilin picked up her skirts, lifted her head regally, and stepped out of hiding.

Chapter 24:

CORMORIN - DECLARING HIS PRINCESS

Governor Fong was doing a remarkable job of telling Prince Cor and Captain Orin precisely nothing. Orin held the big man's hands behind his back, even as Fong's nose continued to bleed down his face and onto his previously resplendent suit, while Cor held the blaster on him.

"Where were you taking these clothes, Fong?" Cor reached with one hand into the case and brought out a fluffy coral dress and a suit to shake them in his face. The suit was at least three sizes too small for the rotund man in front of him. "Somehow I don't think this dress is quite your color."

"It's a gift for Celestine, of course. What do you take me for?"

"And the suits? In two different sizes? Gifts for me, perhaps? Thank you, but I have enough suits, Governor. So let's get back to the EMP blaster." He waved it at him and dropped the clothes. "Where were you going with it? I'm not going to ask you again."

But then, he saw movement out the shuttle bay door windows, on the palace lawn. A girl with long dark hair, a vision in a humongous red dress, sneaking out toward the rocket in its launch tube. It didn't look like… but that sneaking gait was familiar… but it couldn't be….

"What the…? *Meilin?*" Couldn't anyone else see her? But there were no guards or footmen around the rocket any longer, and his men must have been distracted, or enjoying the party. He ground his teeth together at the apparent ineptitude.

Orin turned his head to look, and Fong took the opportunity to slam his head backward into Orin's face and twist out of his hold, diving for Cor. Before Cor could react, Fong was shoving the blaster up with one hand and clocking him across the head with his other, meaty fist. Cor grunted, his head whipping to the side and he went down, retaining just enough sense to roll away from Fong's follow-up kick. He caught the next one, bringing Fong down by rolling into his other leg and slamming his elbow down into the side of his head. Fong went limp.

Cor swore at himself as he dragged himself back to his feet. Orin rolled Fong over and tied his hands with his belt, and Cor looked out at the rocket again. It was her all right. Meilin, though she was clearly wearing some sort of facial disguise. She had just stepped into the tube, quickly opened the rocket door, and was climbing in, ridiculous trailing skirts and all. Someone must have been running interference for her because none of his men seemed to have noticed her.

As quickly as possible, Cor and Orin schlepped Fong back to the Great Room, his nose bleeding profusely, through gaping guests in their finery. It was Cor's decision to throw him at the feet of his mother and some of her guards. They looked up in surprise, having been glued in shock to an apparent princess fight in the middle of the room. A few of the princesses were still rolling around on the floor in their designer puffy dresses, tearing at each other, and yelling highly unladylike obscenities.

The guests watched agape and the vid crew was gleefully filming the action in a circle around the girls. Some of the guards were trying to pry the princesses apart, unfortunately leaving their backs to the windows and patio doors leading out onto the lawn and the rocket.

One of the princesses, Imogen, wriggled free and ran toward Cor. "Help us! Meilin is trying to stop a coup!" One of the guards grabbed her and pushed her to stand with the others in front of the appalled Empress. Cormorin looked around in confusion. Meilin had arranged this? What in the hell was she doing? Now she was trying to *stop* a coup? His heart took a leap of hope.

"Arrest that man," he ordered the Empress's guard who had thankfully found their heads. They grabbed Fong, who was coming around. "For treason to the Crown."

"Cor! What is all this? *What* is going on?" The Empress raised her voice from her throne with her hand to her chest from all the excitement, staring wide-eyed at the behavior of her demure princess candidates, and at Fong.

"I caught *Governor* Fong in the shuttle bay with a classified EMP blaster, Mother, and disguises for, I can only guess, the Rebels in the dungeon who've now gone missing." Orin had received an update on their way to the Great Room. "He is under arrest for treason to the Crown and I will continue questioning him myself—"

He looked past the guests. Meilin's miles of skirt were still trailing out of the rocket. Whose side was she on?

"—just as soon as I take care of another little issue. Orin, find those missing Rebels," Cor ordered and pushed his way through his guests toward the patio doors.

"Yes, Your Highness," Orin answered, motioning to a contingent of guards.

"Cor!" His mother said sharply as the guards hauled Fong away. "What are you doing?"

"I'm not entirely sure, Mother. But I think maybe… I think I may be declaring my Princess!" he yelled as he cleared the guests and broke into a run out the doors. "Who I'm sure has a really good explanation." He hoped.

"Cor!"

But Cor didn't answer. He sprinted toward the rocket, entered the launch tube, and flung the hatch door open.

"Cor!" Meilin gasped, looking up from where she had her hand on the console. "This isn't what it looks like."

"Let me guess, you're trying to stop Fong?"

He couldn't stop himself from grinning when, even through the anti-rec veil, she looked absolutely surprised in a way that told him he was right. Then he realized they didn't have time for banter.

"Are you trying to get yourself killed? Come on Meilin, take that stupid thing off your face. We have to get out of here!" But she just shook her head. "Look, I forgive you. You wanted to poison my mother. I get it. She does that to people. But you had every chance and you didn't do it. Because I know you, Meilin. You're not a killer."

He tried to stare into her eyes through the veil, but couldn't quite see the real girl underneath. He reached up and yanked it off her head. And there was Meilin, looking up at him with no eyebrows, and eyes that were half-worried, half-frantic. He reached for her again, pulling her into his arms. Meilin let herself be pulled forward for a moment, letting him kiss her, really kiss her.

But then she jerked away toward the console. "No! We don't have time for this," she said, but before she could even touch the control panel, there was a click from somewhere inside, and the rocket's electronics whirred to life.

"No, no, no!" said Meilin. "It's not supposed to activate. Who did that?"

"Fong," Cor hissed.

And at the same time Meilin hissed, "Commander Zhang."

He squinted at her. "Whoever it is, there must be a remote switch," said Cor. "We've got to get out of here before they launch this thing." He took her arm.

"No, you don't understand." She shook him off as a robotic voice began to countdown from sixty seconds. "This thing is set to EMP the dome, unless I stop it. You have to get out of here."

He hit the CANCEL LAUNCH button, but it didn't cancel, and the voice kept right on counting down. "Damn." He hit it twice more without result. "EMP the *dome?* What are you talking about?"

"Don't you get it, Cor? The Governor is using the Rebels to install himself as Emperor. As soon as this thing launches, it will collide into the palace dome, and detonate an EMP. With the dome down, the Rebels will attack. Unless I can switch it back to a stupid firework."

"Switch it back? What do you…? How do you…?"

"Because *I* did it Cor. This is my fault. And now I have to fix it."

Chapter 25:

MEILIN - IT'S ALL ABOUT THE ROCKET

"Meilin?" He looked lost.

"I screwed up, Cor. I thought it was you and your mother who killed my family. But now I know it was the Governor, and he's been duping us all along. I switched this thing weeks ago. I made it into an EMP bomb. And now I have to switch it back, if I can. And *you* have to let me. Go Cor, I have to do this."

She shoved him, hard, toward the door and he stumbled. The engines began to rumble as the robotic voice hit ten and continued the countdown. Meilin put her hand back on the console, shut her eyes and felt for the energy that would let her change the programming.

She felt more than saw Cor shake his head. "Not without you. Can't you stop the launch?"

"If I do that now, it'll just explode here." She tried to concentrate, to find the right pathways, but on five he grabbed her and pulled her back toward the door.

"Cor! I have to do this!" Meilin turned and elbowed him in the face, hard, before she wheeled away and put her hand back on the control panel. "Now GO! Get out of here!"

But Meilin would stay. This was her responsibility. If the rocket launched without Meilin changing the trajectory, it would turn around, hit the palace dome, and detonate in an Electro-Magnetic Pulse, bringing down the dome's defenses. The few Rebels inside were only the tip of the iceberg. Hundreds more waited to invade aboard the *Temerity*, hiding on the far side of Gallaius. They would kill the Empress and take her throne, but what Meilin cared about was that they would kill Cor. And install Fong as Emperor. Even if they let Cor live, which Meilin doubted, there was no way that slimy man and his thugs would keep their word. He was the cause of her parent's death, and Lyric's suffering. It would only get worse under an Emperor Fong.

There wasn't time to both change the trajectory and get out. Meilin was going up with the ship.

The countdown hit one.

"Dammit Meilin!" She heard the hatch slam and she felt relief and sadness at once. The rockets fired and though she tried to hold on, she was slammed toward the base of the rocket by the G-forces, into something soft and hard at the same time.

"What do we do now?" Cor asked, still very much present.

She looked around the interior and realized that he'd used the sash from his suit to tie the hatch shut. She couldn't believe he'd stayed.

"Push me up there, to the controls!" she said, vowing to yell at him later. Not that there would be a later. He grabbed her legs and pushed her up toward the console. She squeezed her eyes shut, throwing both hands at the console, sparking her energy through the system. The lights flickered, she pulled back, took a deep breath and tried again, as gently as she could in her haste. They quickly entered weightless space and she found herself pressed against the console and had to push back and hold on at the same time. She focused, this time finding what she needed and pushing the energy through to the guidance and firing systems, just in time to keep them from firing and turning them back toward the Jewel. She finally floated away and Cor wrapped his arms around her, pulling her to him. She collapsed into him, letting go of everything for once and just letting him hold her. What did it matter after all?

"What other surprises do you have for me?" he asked.

"Oh Cor, why did you have to come? Why did you have to stay?" She turned and put her hands to his face as he wrapped her in his arms, feeling as if the oxygen levels were already falling in the cabin.

He smiled softly at her. "I think you know the answer to that. How much time do we have?"

"I don't know for sure. I set it for impact on Gallaius," she returned his smile weakly.

As if he'd gotten a sudden idea more important than holding her until they both passed out, he jerked around, and pushed off to tug a wall panel open. He rummaged through the contents, not finding what he was looking for, before pulling the next panel open and rummaging again.

"What are you doing?" she asked.

"All these old rockets had to have... Yes!" He pulled out two pink, plastic wrapped pouches. He tore the flimsy wrap off the first one to reveal a gooey, stretchy, pink mess. "Bunch up that giant skirt," he ordered. "I don't know how far this will go."

He took out the goop and stretched it and kept stretching, before slapping it over Meilin's head. It felt cold and sticky but she didn't complain, because she didn't have enough air to talk anymore. The edges liked to stick together but he kept stretching until it encased all of her and sealed shut below her feet like a semi-opaque bubble. He took out a little disk from the bag as well, and shoved it into the bubble. It whirred softly and suddenly she could breathe again.

He started doing his own, but he faltered and his movements started to slow. She grabbed it from him and stretched it carefully down over his head, down to his feet. She tried to hurry, but her own bubble made everything sticky, like she was wearing a suit made of tape. She took the disk out of his pouch and, hoping she was doing it right, shoved it into his suit. The whirring started and he began to breathe again. She looked down at her body, covered in opaque pink—the bubble was still blobby, but it had started to conform to her shape.

"It's a pressure stabilization suit." Cor's voice came through the disk that was also delivering the air. "It will convert gases in the rocket into oxygen, for a while. But then we'll be out of luck again."

"It's pink, and it's sticky." She supposed that was the least helpful observation ever, but it was all she had.

"Well, it's probably fifty years old. Be glad it still works. What was your plan? To die in space?" She gave him a look. "Maybe you should have told me about this crazy stunt before and you might've gotten a color choice."

She grunted. "Yeah, while I was locked in the dungeon."

"Well you didn't exactly give me much of a choice, did you?"

She supposed he had a point. "Well, if you're not going to follow my plan to die in space, now what?"

He squinted at her thoughtfully. "How much control do you

have over this thing, like where it lands?"

"You mean crashes and explodes?"

"Yeah, that's no good. How about putting it in orbit? Because I guarantee you my mother will be sending up a rescue crew any minute."

❋ ❋ ❋

It was at least five minutes later, but a small flock of ding-ed-up white mining shuttles launched from Planet Gallaius and surrounded them in space. The three larger ships continued on to enter the dome space-lock on the Jewel's main dome, while two smaller shuttles stayed hovering around the rocket.

"I didn't know there were mining crews on planet today," Cor said.

"Is there some reason why your mother would have called them up to rescue us, rather than transports from the Jewel?"

"I don't know. I just hope there's nothing wrong with the shuttle bay after Fong was in there with an EMP blaster earlier."

She gave him a questioning look.

"I'll tell you about it later." He tried contacting the Jewel, but his com did not go through and he grunted in disgust at the device. They held each other while watching the remaining mining transports fly around them as if trying to figure out how to dock with them. One apparently won out in the rescue effort and a docking tunnel extended from it, like a slow-motion accordion floating in space toward the rocket's door panel.

"Uh," Meilin said after a few attempts to connect the tunnel to the rocket. "They seem to be having some trouble."

"Well, this thing wasn't exactly made to dock with a current day Jewelian transport shuttle. They'll get it."

Cor's com beeped and he grunted in surprise. "Good reception." But it wasn't the transport outside, or the Jewel. He held his com screen out in front of them, hugging her as they were literally stuck together, while they floated in orbit around Gallaius in an antique rocket, as if none of this were that big of a deal. They saw one of Cor's lieutenants on screen, the military encampment on planet Gallaius showing behind her.

"Report," Cor said.

"Your Highness, Princess." The Lieutenant gave a rushed little bow, as if she hadn't heard about, or was ignoring, Meilin's recent stay in the dungeon. "We heard on coms that you are accidentally in space, and a rescue was being launched from the Jewel. Everyone is so pleased that your ship did not blow up."

"Thanks." Cor's response was wry.

"But sir, there's been some strange activity here on the surface. Five mining transports just launched from the forest near the barbarian compound. They're not ours, though." Cor and Meilin stiffened and looked out the window at the transports outside. "We believe they may be the ones that were attacked and lost months ago. They appear headed for the Jewel."

"Uh…" Meilin said.

Cor swore and detached himself from Meilin, looking for a weapon.

"I thought they didn't have the technology to fix them," Meilin said.

"So did I," Cor replied.

"And sir, the Gallaians have been strangely absent today, staying in their underground."

"Shinse." It was Meilin's turn to swear, remembering the strange feeling she'd gotten in the Gallaian underground, and that underground path of increased radiation leading somewhere away from the Gallaian compound. It could have been a tunnel. To the barbarian compound.

Meilin turned to Cor and they stared at each other in horror. "They're in league together," they said at the same time.

And in the next moment, the rocket's hatch door began to open.

"Get to the Jewel!" Cor yelled at his lieutenant. "The barbarians are invading!"

They didn't even see who opened the hatch door, merely the EMP blaster's silver nose-cone that entered first. Meilin grabbed Cor and gripped him tightly through their suits, looking into his face for what could be the last time. What were their chances, unconscious aboard a barbarian ship? And why was it only now that she knew she'd fallen in love with him?

Meilin saw and felt an extreme blast of energy all around, and everything went dark.

ℭhapter 26:

MEILIN - BARBARIAN INVASION

Meilin awoke minutes, or hours later, she didn't know, in a too-bright room, tangled in a mass of red dress and sticky pink suit. She sat straight up, cracking her head against something hard, and hearing a pained grunt that echoed her own. She put a hand to her head, and opened her eyes, blearily seeing Cor above her, leaning away and mirroring her with his hand to his forehead.

"What—what happened?" she asked. She felt drained. They were in the Great Room, and through the glare, the first thing she saw after Cor was an unobstructed view of beautiful blue and green Gallaius, shining through the domed ceiling and huge wall of windows. But it wasn't the Empress sitting on her throne who'd allowed the curtains to be opened wide, and it wasn't Fong either. It was the young Gallaian woman, Sying. And Barbarian leader Skole stood next to her.

On her other side, Fong stood with Celestine, both of them looking outwardly triumphant, though their noses were bandaged and their blackening eyes darted around the room, revealing their uncertainty. The Prince's throne had been removed altogether.

The Empress and princess candidates huddled in the corner nearest Meilin and Cor, surrounded by wild-looking barbarians. Sying's generation of young, apparently ambitious, Gallaians was nearby, keeping an eye on the princesses, but standing cautiously away from the barbarians. The usually pristine moon palace had never seen so much dirt and hair within its walls. The unwashed stench of the barbarians was already thick in the recirculated air and Meilin wondered how long the dome's air filtration system would be able to keep up.

Seeing more of the barbarians than she had ever wanted to see was eye-opening. Their myriad scars and burns, and the lumpy, tumorous growths all over their bodies glowed blue, even in the well-lit room. They gnashed their teeth and growled threateningly at the princesses, making her wonder just how much man was left, or if only animal remained.

Meilin turned her head slightly toward Cor and whispered urgently, "How long before help arrives?"

He gave her a surreptitious welcome back squeeze and a tiny head shake. "She made me order my soldiers to stay out of the dome," he whispered, "or she'd let the barbarians have Mother and the princesses. Our help is stuck in orbit."

She felt her hopes sink. "How did they get in? We stopped the EMP rocket. The Jewel's defenses are still up, right?" If the defenses were down, then the Rebel ship *Temerity* might be able to….

He winced. "They must have been able to use the security codes from the mining transports." They'd never thought the Gallaians would team up with the barbarians, let alone fix the transports and use them to invade.

And then Sying spoke from the Empress's throne. "Ah, you're awake. Yes you, Energy Girl." Meilin heard the Empress and princesses gasp, but she didn't look at them as Cor helped her gently on her feet. "Ah, so he knows now, but they don't. Show them."

When Meilin didn't move to do Sying's bidding, Skole next

to her snarled and took a step toward Meilin. He had one of the new looking, white EMP blasters on his hip, in addition to a large, nasty looking sword strapped to his back, and Cor moved a protective step in front of Meilin, though his own sword scabbard was empty.

Sying put a hand on Skole's dirty, scarred arm and stood, pulling a familiar-looking blue candy from her pocket. She stood close to Skole, his entire attention on her now as she licked the candy and held it up to his mouth. The other barbarians watched enviously as he took it gently, eagerly, from her fingertips, and she reached up to give him a sensuous kiss with the candy. Meilin threw up a little in her mouth.

Some of the other Gallaians had looks of disgust on their faces as well, but they merely watched their leader and the barbarian.

"But, they *hunted* your people," Meilin couldn't help saying in disgust.

"They did, Energy Girl." Sying turned back to her. "For years and years while the Royals turned a blind eye up here on their moon, and you Lyrans too, on your perfect planet." Her eyes flashed in anger. "Since then, we've learned the power of our glorious, shining fruits. And now, *we* are the hunters." She delicately wiped her mouth, and Skole looked on her, dulled and enraptured.

"Still they are, shall we say, ravenous. Difficult to control when they don't get what they crave." The threat to the Empress and princesses was heavy in the air. The other barbarians had not gotten theirs and they growled in disapproval. The princesses shied back.

"And now, I asked you to show us what you can do with that Gift of yours, Energy Girl. Impress me, and I may allow you to join us." Sying paused. "I won't ask again."

Glaring at Sying, but not seeing another way, Meilin held out her hand and tried to call the energy, but Meilin felt oddly numb and depleted. It was like the last EMP hit she'd taken had gone straight through her, flipping an off switch she hadn't known she'd possessed. Her hand sparked a little but no more, and she dropped it to her side, frustrated.

"I can't."

Sying grunted, unimpressed, and waved her hand. "Throw them in the dungeon for now until I decide what to do with them. Meanwhile, bring the vid crew back. The Empress has an address to give." The barbarians grinned and advanced on their captives, Meilin, Cor, and the princesses, separating the Empress and shunting her toward Sying and Skole. Fong, who'd merely watched in silence the whole time, perked up in anticipation, and Celestine beside him.

"Take her too." Sying motioned toward Celestine.

"Hey, we had a deal," Fong blustered and tried to step protectively in front of his daughter, but she squeaked as several grinning barbarians herded her toward the other princesses. Celestine found Kaletra and tried to hug her in fear, but Kaletra pushed her away.

Sying turned cold eyes on Governor Fong. "You have proved worthless in our dealings. You were supposed to get the dome defenses down, but you did not. Thankfully we had a plan *B*."

"Well, I… what about disabling the Prince's droid army? Who do you think did that?" Fong puffed his chest.

But Sying wasn't dumb. "I think the few Lyran Rebels you brought to the moon did that, despite your ineptitude. I shall thank *them* when I deal with them. And, thanks to your failure to get the dome's defenses down, the rest of your Rebel protectors are out there, not in here." She pointed out the glass dome and Meilin sighed. It was true. Thanks to her, Commander Zhang, the *Temerity*, and her crew were out there somewhere, probably hiding out behind Gallaius. If Meilin had allowed the rocket to EMP the dome, at least the *Temerity* and her crew would be here now. They'd be trying to install Fong, but apparently all Meilin's efforts had only made bad worse. She knew what was logically coming.

"Kill him," Sying ordered. Skole and at least a dozen barbarians advanced on Fong, grinning that they were finally being allowed to kill someone. The others watched, growling and grinding their teeth. "Not here, not here!" she amended. "Take him outside. The last thing we need is blood showing up in the video." They glanced at her and obediently dragged Fong out the glass doors, across the patio and onto the lawn. Skole drew his huge, black sword and Meilin looked away, unable to watch. She heard Celestine's muffled scream and knew Fong's attempted rise to power was over.

"Now then, that's been taken care of," Sying's voice rang through the nearly silent room. "Take the Prince and his wannabe princesses to the dungeon."

Six barbarians herded them toward the inner doors and the princesses whimpered. The frenetic looks on the barbarian's slobbering faces said they would have a fight to get to the dungeons intact. Meilin readied herself, kicking off her silly heels and digging her toes into the stone for grip. She felt almost nothing through her Gift, only a bit of the palace's energy through the soles of her feet. Numbed.

"Sying, Your Highness," a young Gallaian man said quietly, some unspoken message exchanging between himself and Sying.

"Oh, fine." Sying drew out a full bag of blue candies and threw them to the young man, who had the immediate attention of every barbarian in the room. They advanced on him and he quickly tossed candies out in a shower of blue. Meilin heard the Empress whimper again, but no candies came her way. And then they were herded out the doors.

Chapter 27:

CORMORIN - TO THE DUNGEON

This day was *not* going as planned. Prince Cor was being led to his own dungeon under the military complex by a gang of well-armed, cannibalistic barbarians for whom today was like New Year's Day. Mildly controlled and satiated with the candy, they strutted with shiny new swords and white blasters on their hips from a raid on his armory when they'd arrived, taking control of the Jewel and her military capabilities. He wondered if most of them even knew how to use the new weapons.

He was kicking himself. He should have found a way to bomb the barbarians when they'd had the chance, but oh no, Mother had wanted to save and recover the Terran digital data that might remain in the barbarian stronghold. They had waited impotently for an opportunity to present itself, one that never came. And all the while they'd bled contract miners and ships to barbarian raids.

He and Meilin were now unarmed in the middle of a coup with a group of civilian princess hostages to look after, and Meilin unable to do whatever shocking, tazing thing she had done before. He saw her Gift spark impotently at her fingertips, her hands tied tightly behind her back as she walked ahead of him, but she seemed unable to wield the energy.

"How did you get out the last time?" Cor whispered to her, working at the bonds that tied his hands while they walked, but the nearest of their four remaining barbarian guards heard him and whacked him upside the head with his shiny new energy pistol. Cor grunted at the pain in his ear and kept walking. They'd lost two of their barbarian "guards" who'd apparently gotten their hands on too many of the blue candies, but it looked like the others weren't going to follow suit. The barbarian strutted by Cor and Meilin to leer at the princesses. Moments later, he saw the girls pull away, one by one with outraged squeals of disgust at the barbarian's dirty, groping hands.

"Hey! Leave them alone!" Cor commanded, but the guard just sneered and ignored him. Cor kept working on his bonds behind his back.

"Yun broke us out," Meilin replied in a whisper. "You know, my maid? Yeah, she wasn't really my maid. Wish I knew what happened to her." Meilin sounded worried.

He grunted at the admission. When this was all over, he and Meilin would get to the bottom of everything that was happening and why, but for now, he had to get them out of this. And now three of the four barbarians were hassling the princesses. He felt the knot slip a little on the rope at his wrists.

They arrived at the well-lit dungeon and one of the barbarians held the door open, ushering the princesses through, all the while leering at them. The other two herded the princesses forward, touching and stroking the soft skin on their exposed arms and shoulders on their way past, left bare by their fancy dresses. The princesses yelled and hit at them to keep their hands to themselves, but the barbarians seemed to take that as a challenge. The "guard" looked like they had every intention of following the girls into the cell.

It took Cor a minute through his outrage to realize, there

ought to be a dozen Rebels in that holding cell. The fourth barbarian, who seemed a little less distracted by the princesses, noticed something on the floor and bent to pick it up. Cor recognized the mechanical padlock in his hands that had been supposed to keep Meilin in the cell. The barbarian looked sharply at the empty white room and began to say something to the other three groping guards, but what it was none of them would ever know.

With all the barbarians distracted, Cor took the opening. He ripped his hands free and came down with an elbow to the barbarian's neck who was kneeling on the floor. Meilin must have had the same instinct because at the same time, she stepped forward and kicked viciously up into the barbarian's chin. Struck by the two blows from opposite directions, the barbarian's neck gave a horrible snap, and he went down, never to get back up. The other three, distracted barbarians whipped around at the noise, pulling blasters from their waistbands. Cor jumped in front of Meilin and pushed one blaster up, punching that dirty hairy face and grabbing the sword from the sheath on the barbarian's hip, but he knew it wouldn't be enough with two other blasters pointed at Meilin.

A blast went harmlessly into the ceiling and the lights went out, leaving them in the eerie blue glow from the barbarians. But instead of more energy blasts, like he was expecting, he heard the yell of war cries echoing from the guard station down the hall. The barbarians swung around to face the escaped Rebels, but were too late.

When the princesses had stopped screaming, Cor stood with one of his favorite *miaodao* in his hand, taken from the sheath on the back of a now-dead barbarian. He held it at the ready toward the Rebels. The two front Rebels had swords of their own, one a man with a *dadao*, a big, curved broadsword, and the other a woman with two light *jian*. The other Rebels had grabbed the blasters and they all held the weapons at the ready on Cor and Meilin, whose hands were still tied. To his surprise, she spun around to stand with the Rebels, her back and bound wrists to the female Rebel with the two light swords.

"Don't cut me with those things, Sumai," she ordered.

"Meilin!" he gasped, and he knew a look of pure betrayal must show on his face. The Rebels grinned.

Chapter 28:

MEILIN - THE EMPRESS ABDICATES HER THRONE

As soon as her bonds were cut, Meilin took one of the light *jian*—and spun back around, to stand at Cor's side.

"Meilin!" It was the Rebels' turn to gasp in outrage. "Traitor!" She saw Xiaobo, Sumai, and Li at the front of the group. They must have finished taking out the droids in the armory and come back here to wait for the EMP that never came.

"Everyone calm down," she said, but kept her new sword at the ready. "We're all on the same side now, believe it or not."

"Oh, we are, huh? With *him?*" Xiaobo sneered at Cor. "So who were they?" she nodded at the dead barbarians at their feet.

"Gallaian barbarians," Meilin answered. "Fong, the one *you* would install as Emperor, was in league with them. He's dead now."

"*What?* You're lying." Sumai squinted at her.

"Am I? Fong never came for you, did he?" she asked. "The rocket launched early, and there was no EMP, was there?" She didn't mention that part of that was her doing, of course. "And he left you here to rot in the dungeons."

The looks on their faces confirmed it. "Something must have gone wrong," Sumai shook her head stubbornly. "We were just coming to find out what had happened up there when you came walking in with these dirtballs."

Cor snorted at her side but Meilin gave him a look and he held his tongue. "I'll tell you what happened. The dome's defenses are still up, so Commander Zhang and the rest of the Rebels are still out in orbit. The Gallaians found a way in though, and have taken over the Jewel with their barbarian dogs as enforcers. With Fong's help for the past several months, they've been drugging the Empress, and are forcing her to abdicate her throne as we speak. Their deal, I think, was that Fong was going to take over rule of Lyric, but now the Gallaian leader, Sying, is taking over everything."

"That—that can't be…" Sumai stammered while the rest of the Rebels looked horrified.

"You're making this up," Xiaobo said. *"He's* brainwashed you, Wei." He pointed at Cormorin. *"He* killed our families, or don't you remember? Is avenging their deaths no longer important to you?" He advanced on Cor with murder in his eyes and that big, curved broadsword in his hands. In answer, Cor brought up his long sword.

But Meilin jumped in front of him – and *lowered* her own sword.

"Meilin!" Cor hissed in fear as Xiaobo brought the tip of his sword up to her throat. She forced herself to stand her ground.

"I have not forgotten my family, or any of the others who died," she said quietly. Though they'd never been close, they were comrades, and she looked him in the eye. If she couldn't get through to him, they stood no chance. "But Cor is not responsible. He was a child, like us, when the plague hit. Even his mother, who I held responsible, is not fully to blame. She sent doses of the cure to Lyric in good faith, enough for everyone. It was Fong who put a price on that cure, who sold it on the black market for profit. But that doesn't mean the Empress is blameless. She was in charge. Fong was *her* appointee and he went rogue on her watch. But as much as we don't like her, we can't let this Sying and her irradiated barbarians take over Lyric. Come with us. See that I'm telling the truth."

Slowly, Xiaobo lowered his sword, though his nostrils still flared in anger.

"Fine," he said. "We will go see. But one wrong move, out of either of you…" he trailed off but let his eyes communicate the threat. He kept his sword at the ready.

"You first, Prince," he sneered. "Then you, traitor," he said to Meilin, gesturing with a tiny flick of the tip of his wide, curved sabre. Cor started to lead the way back up to the Great Room with Meilin following.

"What about us?" someone called behind them. Meilin looked back to see Imogen, Orencia and the other princesses still inside the open cell, barbarian bodies littered the floor near the doorway. She'd almost forgotten about the princesses.

"It'll be safest for you here," she said. "Lock yourselves in. We'll come back for you when this is all over." At least, Meilin hoped they would. She continued down the corridor after Cor.

"What are we up against?" she asked him. "I counted five transports. How many barbarians should we expect?"

"The smallest two could hold probably ten max. The soil-haulers, I don't know, twenty, maybe twenty-five barbarians."

"So, we're talking a hundred, at most?"

He nodded. Meilin counted. "And there are fifteen of us. Whew." She released a breath.

"The armory held drones, droids, and Light Plasma Blasters, whose default setting is stun, but that can be changed if they figure out how. And also a few Augmented EMP Rifles, harmful to electronics—and Meilin. These swords came from the armory, so we're going to have to see how heavily it's guarded, and what's left for us," Cor said grimly.

Sneaking back through the underground halls, toward the palace, they managed to avoid a few half-stoned barbarians. Too bad they couldn't expect them all to be that way. They carefully stepped into the armory, and surprisingly found it unmanned. The reason for this, however, became clear when they saw that all the drones, and battle droids, had been incapacitated with an EMP blast. All the blasters and EMP rifles were gone, and most of the swords too.

They took what they could salvage, and regretfully, Meilin handed off her sharp, fast, *jian* to a Rebel who was otherwise unarmed, but she took a metal bo staff for herself, and they continued on toward the Great Room, realizing quickly that this was where all the barbarians congregated.

Meilin pointed up. "The balcony," she whispered and led the way to the servants' staircase. Meilin felt a strong sense of déjà vu as she crouched behind the same potted greenery to observe what was going on below.

The Empress was standing now, her back to the glass doors to the Palace dome's patio and lawn, planet Gallaius shining behind her. She had a blank look on her face and glassy eyes as she addressed a holo-cam drone, and through it, her subjects.

"My people, today was meant to be a day of joy, but instead, it is with great sadness that I must inform you that your Prince, my son, Cormorin, was fatally wounded today in a tragic rocket accident. I cannot tell you how broken-hearted I am." She paused and appeared to try to collect herself. "For the welfare of the commonwealth, I am taking a leave of absence to grieve."

Meilin turned to Cor with one eyebrow raised at the news of his death, but he just looked immensely sad at how far his mother had fallen. The look was echoed in the face of every palace guest and every servant who now stood around the edge of the giant room, witnessing the Empress's coerced, drugged announcement. She counted only about twenty barbarians within her sight, staying out of range of the camera drone and she wondered how many were directly under their balcony, and where the others could be.

"I cannot think of a more fitting appointment to lead us during my absence, than the honorable Sying, head of Gallaian recovery efforts." The comparatively inelegant Gallaian woman stepped up on the Empress's side, now dressed in borrowed, ill-fitting finery. She bowed solemnly to the camera. "With her leadership, I have no doubt that Gallaius and Lyric will be in good hands during my absence, and when I return, we shall continue our most important work, because we must, without our beloved Prince Cor. Thank you." The two women bowed to the camera and the Empress signed off with tears in her eyes. Did she believe what she had just now told her people? It was hard to tell.

"Thank you, Ming-Zhu. What a lovely and heartfelt message," Sying said with a cold smile and presented the Empress with a large bag of blue candies. The Empress's face lit up like a child just given her most desired present and she immediately ripped off a wrapper and began stuffing candies into her face, one, two, three of them. And her mouth clearly began to glow blue from the inside.

"Slow down, Ming-Zhu. We wouldn't want you to have a bad reaction. Now what do you say?"

The Empress mumbled something that sounded vaguely like "thank you" as her head began to loll around her neck.

"Thank you, who?" Sying pressed, and slapped the Empress across the face.

"Thank you, Empress Sying," the Empress mumbled and there was a gasp around the room.

"Yes. That is what we all needed to hear," Sying purred and turned to the palace staff gathered around the room. "Your prince is dead, his guards have been dealt with, and the Empress has now clearly abdicated her throne to me. So you have a choice. Bow before me, declare your loyalty, and you may stay. Anyone who does not, may leave," she smiled, "via the airlock." She waited as one by one, they all bowed to her. The new Empress's barbarian dogs hooted and clapped while Sying smiled triumphantly. She unwrapped another candy and stuffed it in the Empress's freely drooling, glowing, blue mouth, and watched as the Empress slumped to the floor.

hapter 29:

MEILIN - BATTLE

Meilin watched the events below unfold alongside Cor and the Rebels. She gripped Cor's hand. Hold it together, Cor. *Hold it together,* she thought desperately at him. They needed some kind of plan.

But Cor jumped up and ran to the railing. "Mother!" he yelled. "She's lying! I'm alive and here! Spit those things out!"

Or, we could go off half-cocked and see where that gets us. The crowd below erupted at the sight of their beloved Prince Cor, returned from the dead. He grabbed the rope, still attached to the railing that had held the rocket earlier—and jumped over the rail, swinging down and pushing his way past the nearest barbarian.

"Shinse! Go, go, go!" Meilin shouted at the Rebels. If they didn't move fast, they were going to get pinned down up here. She saw the new, self-declared Empress bring up a blaster with the distinctive EMP nose cone and point it at the balcony. Instead of following Cor over the railing, Meilin and the Rebels dove for the back servants' stairs and sprinted as quietly as possible down them.

They heard shouts of "Get them!" and "Bring me the energy girl! I just heard her," from Sying. Meilin rolled her eyes. That woman had so much to learn about the etiquette of being an Empress. She could hear barbarians thundering up the richly carpeted main staircase.

And meanwhile, Meilin needed her Gift to work again. Holding her bo staff in one hand, she devoted as much of her concentration as possible while going down the stairs to calling up an energy ball in the palm of her hand. She sparked and fizzled at random spots around her body, but no energy ball. Crap.

She hadn't realized how much she'd come to depend on her Gift until she didn't have it. She wondered how Cor was doing, alone against a hundred barbarians, and she forgot her fear and flew the rest of the way down the stairs, followed by the Rebels. She peered out the door to the ante room cautiously, hearing the barbarians still barreling up the main stairs. She gestured to the Rebels behind her.

"Come on!" She dashed on tiptoe across the carpeted ante-room to the double doors of the Great Room. She held up a hand for the Rebels to stop behind her, and peeked in. Cor was kneeling next to his mother at the center of the wooden dance floor, pulling blue goop out of her mouth while a dozen barbarians held energy blasters on him and dozens more circled.

The cone-nosed EMP rifle was still in the hands of Sying, pointed at the balcony. "Well?" she yelled up to her barbarians.

"No one here!" came the bellowed reply.

And below, Meilin and the Rebels barged into the Great Room.

She drove one end of her bo into the gut, and then up into the chin of the big barbarian in her way, before whirling and cracking the next two in the side of the head before they realized what was happening. She spun and danced with her bo, her comrades working over the surprised barbarians closest to them with her. But their advantage of surprise was quickly over, again, and the barbarians brought their blasters up to bear.

Meilin dodged, using the pillars for cover as guests and servants ran for the doors. She remembered what Cor had said, and prayed the blasters were still set to stun. But she had to get to Cor.

She heard only a few blasts before she heard Sying screech in indignation, "Don't shoot my subjects!" The blasts into the ducking and running civilians stopped.

Cor was up now, defending his mother with his long sword and a blaster he'd gotten off one of the barbarians. He aimed at Sying but two barbarians jumped between them, attacking Cor, and she hid behind a post. Skole left her side and advanced on Cor with his own great sword, while Cor was busy with the two crazy-eyed barbarians.

"Cor, behind you!" Meilin yelled, but then she was busy again herself. There were so many of them, too many to count, but there had to have been more than fifty barbarians in that room, under the balcony and out of sight of the camera drone while the Empress made her statement. She found a whole circle of barbarians around her and saw with a quick glance around the room that Cor and each of the Rebels were similarly engaged.

And then, through the fleeing crowd of palace guests and staff, in snuck the princesses. *What* were they doing there? Meilin had been trying to get to the center of the room to help Cor and the Empress, who he'd propped hastily up against a pillar, but now she had a dozen wayward princesses to worry about too? They were supposed to stay in the dungeons, where it was safe!

The Princesses fanned out from the door, wearing their gorgeous, though impractical, voluminous rainbow of dresses with even less practical high heels. Meilin had admired the fancy, shiny shoes with them when they'd arrived two days earlier; pairs of boots with lacy cutouts in the top-grain leather, or spike heeled slippers studded with jewels. But now, though her own bare footedness was less than ideal, she was worried their fancy heels would trip them up.

She heard high-pitched cries of, "Oh my!" and "Don't hurt me. I must be in the wrong place!" At the same time, Meilin saw blurs of brightly colored dresses whisking and spinning this way and that, the owners with their arms up in apparent panic. *What* were they doing? Meilin had her own fight to concentrate on, but her opponents, and everyone in the room, slowed at the sight of those confused, colorful, *panicked* girls, looking like tropical birds trapped in a room full of dirty barbarians. The girls were *distracting* the barbarians, she realized, and what was more unbelievable—it was working.

The barbarians paused at the fairytale beauty before them, seeming confused and mesmerized by the swirling, sparkling volumes of fabric. Their confusion only grew when the fluttering of those soft, fluffy skirts against their legs turned into unexpected pain. The fancy spike-heeled shoes and boots, sparkling in the light from the chandeliers, kicked and stomped into dirty barbarian feet, knees, and softer parts. Other girls had broken the heels off their slippers and were wielding the impossibly spiked, metal tipped heels like the micro-batons from the practice room, in spinning fist strikes to necks, faces, ears, and eyes.

Meilin felt like a proud mama, watching her girls fight like furies, turning to each other's aid as needed. She watched a fast, flawless high kick by Orencia into an unsuspecting barbarian throat and nearly cheered.

And then she nearly fell victim to the mesmerizing sight of the princesses herself. A whistling energy coming toward her was the only thing that saved her and Meilin spun away, barely blocking a barbarian attacker in time. The swirling fabric of her own red and gold skirt was help and hindrance both, as it took a glancing sword strike instead of her body, but at the same time she had to keep sweeping it out of her way in a constant, extra dance step that hindered her movement at the worst times. The length of her bo helped her keep barbarians at a distance, until that is, her skirt got pinned with a barbarian broad sword, stuck into a lucky crack in a stone pillar, stopping her forward momentum and tripping her, sending her bo flying to clatter five feet away.

The barbarian closest to her grinned at unarming her and she ducked the meaty fist he swung past her ear. She grabbed the hilt of the ugly two-handed broad sword that pinned her to the column. She swung under it, the leverage freeing it from the stone and she allowed the momentum to bring her around, swinging the heavy sword up in a debilitating slice through the barbarian's stomach muscles. He fell and she wasted no time in taking the sword to the large, hanging swath of her skirt, before it could get her killed.

As she ripped and sawed at the unexpectedly sturdy fabric and seams, her back to the column, she felt more than saw the energy of another strike coming at her side, fast, and jumped back, blocking badly. It was a one-handed block with the heavy two-handed sword, and it was knocked clean from her grasp with a painful jar to her wrist. Left only with the long swath of red and gold fabric in her hands, she looked up and saw who was attacking her—Sying.

She dodged the light, single-handed, double-edged *jian* and caught the next strike with the fabric, wrapping the sword and spinning her body, yanking it down, and hoping to free it from its wielder. But Sying skillfully kept her grip and sliced through the layers of fabric, and Meilin realized this might've worked better on a primitive barbarian sword. Meilin dove for her bo staff.

"So, *sister*. You turned out to be a disappointment."

"As have you," Meilin replied, rolling to her feet with her bo in hand to face Sying.

"You should have said yes when I gave you the chance to join us."

"Oh? I don't remember. Was that before or after you made out with Skole?"

Sying made a face and Meilin knew she'd hit home. "They are a means to an end. I thought you understood. I thought you hated the Royals as much as we do. They bombed our world and then abandoned us to die. No pretty words from the Prince, or deliveries of food and soldiers to 'protect' us will make that go away. We had to find a way to protect ourselves."

"But the barbarians have spent years attacking you, hunting your people!"

"And then we overcame, because we had no choice. They can't hurt us anymore; they *serve* us. We learned to control the barbarians, as we will control the Royals. We will take what should be ours, and leave them to die, as they did to my people. As they did to *your* family. And we will share the healthy planet of Lyric, as we should have all along."

They clashed again, still circling and Meilin shook her head. "But it was Fong, not the Royals who withheld medicine from Lyric. I'm sorry they abandoned your people. The Empress should have helped you as soon as she found out there were survivors. What they did was inexcusable. But Cor is trying to make amends—"

"It is too late for amends!" Sying cut her off. "And if you're with the Royals, then you're against us."

"And if you're with the barbarians, *you're* against *us*," Meilin replied, and sword and bo clashed again, discussion over.

As she and Sying danced around each other, over and around fallen barbarian bodies, it was a serious disadvantage that Meilin was barefoot. She constantly felt a distinct *ew* factor, and knew she'd have to deal with finding shoes as soon as no one was trying to slice her head off. But first she had to try not to get hit by rogue blaster fire, especially of the EMP variety.

Meilin felt like she was dodging blows and blasts on all sides, yet she couldn't resist mocking Sying. "So, Skole. Gross, huh? How's that to wake up to?"

Sying merely scowled at her, and Meilin took a split-second opening to spin her bo around her body and direct it at her opponent's head. However, when one of the electric blasts flying around them hit her bo staff, a mere inch from Sying's head, electricity ran up the metal into her hands, tazing Sying at the same time. She dropped to the floor in spasms, and Meilin dropped her bo.

"Gah!" She shook out her numb hands. The next barbarians came at her, several at a time now, seemingly mad about the fall of their Gallaian Empress. Meilin threw a spinning kick up into her opponent's face before diving past another for her bo again. She grabbed it and rolled, feeling the remaining energy give her a shock through the metal. Adrenaline coursed through her veins and into her brain, and something clicked into place, through her synapses, rerouting what had been broken. Her hands sparked on her bo and she spun in a circle, holding the staff at one end, out at the barbarians now surrounding her. A flash issued from the end of it, so bright and so fast that the barbarians were blasted back, one after the other, going down like dominoes struck by lightning.

She looked at her bo in surprise to see it now wrapped in a ribbon of energy, like a glowing spiral helix. She'd never had that happen before. A rush of relief hit and she grinned, blasting a barbarian off his feet from ten paces. She was back.

She worked her way toward Cor and found herself back to back with him, surrounded by a horde of barbarians wielding black pitted broadswords.

Unfortunately, blaster hits only slowed them a few seconds and fueled their anger. Some of the ones who'd been blasted were even now getting up, and a few seemed inspired by Meilin and her bo. They strapped their blasters to swords, whipping them through the air and making fearsome, electrocuting swords. She started gathering her energy to throw.

Those cut down by a blaster sword, or Meilin's electrified bo were not getting back up. They were down to about half the original number of barbarians, but also, half the number of Rebels remained standing.

And then, Cor went down. Hit by an electrified sword, he was blasted back into a large pillar, where Meilin was sure she saw his head crack hard against the stone before he fell to the floor.

"Cor!" Meilin screamed and she felt all the energy she was building up to throw instead just—burst—out through her very pores, like a giant ball of light all around her body that exploded outward in a mighty flash of light and energy. She fell by Cor's side.

At first, she thought she'd passed out, but the darkness she saw was from the palace itself. The only light to be seen was coming from the stars outside, and the barbarians blue glow. Their energy whips and swords stopped abruptly with the power outage. They couldn't see Meilin or the Rebels, and the glowing barbarians had to pause and look for dark, shadowy targets.

Meilin bent over Cor, feeling for a pulse. Was he alright? His pulse was thread, but there, and she found a freely bleeding gash on his head and a bad slice on his arm. She ripped some fabric from the bottom of her dress and pressed it to his wound. He didn't make a sound.

"Cor, come on Cor," she whispered, but the closest glowing barbarian must have heard her. She saw glowing, grinning teeth and an eerily glowing shape come toward her, arms raised as if he held a sword or weapon overhead. Emotionless, she brought up an energy ball and blasted him across the room before going back to Cor. And invisible ninjas seemed to descend on the blue glowing barbarians. A few at a time they fell, until they were all down. Some of them leaked blue glowing blood that illuminated their bodies strangely. Meilin saw some lighter blue figures running out the Great Room doors, but she let them go. She had to make sure Cor would be alright.

An emergency generator kicked on, and there he was, lying amidst the carnage looking pale as a ghost with part of her red silk dress tied around his head. She grabbed his com earpiece, pinching his ear probably harder than she needed to, but he didn't wake and his com didn't burble its usual welcome tone.

Could it be? She'd EMP'd the whole room, the whole palace? She concentrated on finding the energy paths inside the little com device attached to his ear. *Deep breaths,* she whispered to herself; calm. On the third breath, she found what she was looking for, a little burned out glitch in the wiring. She formed a splint around it, rerouting the signal, and she stuffed it in her own ear. This time when she pressed it, she heard static, and then Lieutenant Orin's voice came over the Com.

"Prince Cor, are you there? Answer me!" he sounded frantic.

"Orin, it's me, Meilin," she said. "Get down here, quick. Cor's down, he and the Empress both need a medic. Most of the barbarians are down. The Princesses are safe, I think. But some of the Gallaians have escaped. I think you'll find them in the transport bay trying to take off. Arrest them."

There was a pause as Orin digested all that. "Yes, Princess Meilin," was all he said.

Chapter 30:

MEILIN - AFTER THE FIGHT

Cor's security forces returned from their enforced orbit and immediately locked the Jewel down. Sying's remaining Gallaian entourage were captured and imprisoned, awaiting trial for treason and murder of the Empress, who had been found after the battle, her throat slit by a barbarian sword. The autopsy found that her radiation levels were off the charts and concluded she had been taking the blue candies for far longer than a few days. Cor was heartbroken.

He received thirty stitches in his arm, but refused pain meds, instead gripping Meilin's hand on his good side, and giving orders from his hospital bed shoring up the Jewel's defenses and calling his forces on Gallaius home immediately. No one else was allowed in or out, not even the stranded celebration guests until their statements were taken and they were cleared of any involvement in the coup, one by one.

It was late into the night when enough was known that Cor could address his people. But instead of waiting for morning and a few hours' sleep, with his head and arm bandaged and in a sling, Cor held a press conference. He seemed nervous and asked Meilin to stand by his side in front of the camera. The drone cam pilot counted down, holding his fingers in the air, 3, 2, 1, and Cor was on, Meilin standing impotently at his side, wondering what she was doing there.

"Citizens, whether you are Lyran, Jewelian, or Gallaian, as

you can see, my mother the Empress was greatly mistaken when she announced my death. The truth however, is much more tragic than a simple mistake. This evening, at approximately seven o'clock local time, there was a catastrophic attack on the Jewel, an attempted coup. My mother the Empress, it saddens me greatly to say, was killed in the attack, which is still undergoing a thorough investigation.

"It appears that the Empress, unknown to her or anyone else, was being drugged by ex-Governor Fong of Lyric and a band of Gallaians led by a woman named Sying, the previously unknown leader of the barbarians. As such, the Empress was unaware of the statements they forced her to make. I want to assure you that the Jewel and her civilians are safe, largely due to a surprising ally, the Lyran Rebels."

He paused to let that nugget explode in listeners' craniums before turning to Meilin and continuing. "Princess Meilin and I discovered the plot by Governor Fong and his Gallaian allies. Though no one believed her at first, Meilin refused to sit back and allow Fong to declare himself the ruler of Lyric, which was his goal. We also discovered that he had been stealing from the Crown and the Lyran people for years, and was responsible for an unknown number of plague victims not receiving plague medication. This knowledge sits heavy within my heart. Though he did not survive today's insurrection, I give you my word that his actions will be thoroughly investigated and reparations made, to the best of the Crown's ability.

"With the unexpected but nevertheless invaluable help of a group of Lyran Rebels, and the Princess candidates who remained loyal throughout, Fong and the Gallaian barbarians were defeated today. I am saddened at the great losses we sustained. We not only lost my mother, the Empress, but we also lost friends and allies who died fighting for what was right. I will be forever grateful for their sacrifice. I ask you to bow your heads with me in a moment of silence."

He paused for a long minute before turning to Meilin. "I am also grateful for the tenacity and courage of this woman standing next to me, Princess and Lyran, Wei Meilin. Without her, I would not be standing here, and today's outcome would have been wholly different.

"My mother, the Empress, during these last several months of her life, was insistent that I choose a bride and marry. As you may know, she even went so far as to recruit fifteen girls from Lyric with royal blood and bring them here for me to choose from. As with many a ruler before her, she wouldn't take no for an answer, though I did my best to tell her no on several occasions.

"Because that didn't work, as anyone who knew her could attest, I was going to go through with the process and when it came time to announce my decision, which was supposed to have been tonight, I was going to kindly but firmly say that I couldn't possibly choose. I would say that each of these young women were so brilliant, kind, articulate, accomplished, and lovely, that choosing between them was impossible, and leave it at that. That was my plan anyway.

"And, I know," he cleared his throat and looked at Meilin, suddenly seeming unsure of himself as he looked into her eyes,

"Meilin, I know you didn't come here with any intent of marriage. And while I didn't think I was ready to get married myself, Meilin I'm sure of it now. You are my match." He got down on one knee and she felt her heart jump in her chest. Despite herself she began to tear up and put her hand to her heart.

"I know I'm putting you on the spot, and my timing couldn't be more terrible. I hope you'll forgive me. I don't even have a ring picked out because I want you to choose a ring you'll be happy to wear the rest of your life. But please, say you'll stay here with me, and become my bride, my chosen princess."

She choked up, looking in his eyes, and couldn't answer for a few moments as he smiled up at her hopefully. And then she shook her head and whispered, "I'm sorry, Cor. I can't."

His hopeful look fell and he stood up, clearing his throat. She could see him close down. "Well, I guess that's that then." He turned away, but she caught his good arm and yanked him back.

"I want to! Can't you see that?" She swiped at the tears that refused to dry. "And damn you for doing this in public, in front of the cameras we both hate! But I am *Lyran first!* Before what I want."

"What do you want, Meilin?" he asked, and everything she'd been wishing for the people of her planet tumbled out.

"I want elections for my people, Cor!" she blurted. He looked shocked and she realized how that sounded. "Elected representatives who are responsible and answerable, not *only* to you and the Crown, but to the people of Lyric.

"Fong did not answer to us, he did not represent us, he lied to you, and took advantage of us all." She took a deep breath.

"Can't you see? I *want* to stay with you." She finally released his arm. "But I must return home. If it is at all within my power, Cor, I will ensure free and fair elections for my people. You have to know that it's the only way we can move forward from this. So I ask you," she paused and took a deep breath, drawing herself up and knowing that if she hadn't crossed the line already, she was about to. "No. I demand, as a citizen and a Lyran, free and fairly elected representatives to represent our needs and concerns to the Crown. Otherwise, what did we just fight for?" She bit her lip, knowing she'd gone too far, but forced herself to stand her ground, feeling completely bare to him and the world. Unarmed physically and emotionally.

Through all this, he'd looked shocked. And then thoughtful. She felt hope blossom in her. It was within his power to deny her everything, to imprison her for daring to demand anything of him. And yet, he merely raised an eyebrow.

"Now that's a tall order," he said, and she could see his brain working, and she loved him even more that he didn't cut off the cameras, and throw her in the dungeon once more. Instead he nodded. "We shall need to work out the details of course, but I agree. On one condition."

At this point she felt she would promise him anything, but she forced herself to contain that gut reaction. It was her turn to raise an eyebrow.

"*You* will be my appointed representative for Lyric until the elections can take place, no more than three months from today," he said.

She was shocked and he looked straight at the camera drone.

"Make no mistake, Lyran citizens, this woman saved us all today, through her courage and sheer grit. She saved not only my life, against all odds, but every life here on the Jewel, and many more on Lyric that would have been lost if the Gallaians and barbarians had been able to take over. And if you couldn't tell, she is fiercely loyal to Lyric." He smiled at her and she felt her heart melt. "She will serve the Crown well, but moreover, she will serve her people well."

She hesitated, finding herself embarrassed by the praise. And then she nodded acceptance. It was more than she could have hoped for.

Chapter 31:

MEILIN - THREE MONTHS LATER

Three months later, Meilin was living on Lyric, in a small house newly built on her parents' land. Cor had instated reparations for Lyrans, Rebels included, which meant returning the land confiscated under Fong.

Elections day had come like a freight train the day before. She'd spent it with her team, including Yun, Imogen, and Orencia, in their office, the newly formed Lyran Office of Elections Integrity, watching the returns and checking with voting locations around the globe to ensure that adult Lyrans had the right and opportunity to vote for their district's elected representative. By all reports it had gone well, without a single contested race. They'd spent the evening celebrating, before she returned home to her empty little house.

The next day, she took the first day off she'd had in weeks, and she wasn't sure what to feel. Ecstatic that the woman who won her own newly drawn electoral district seemed like an honestly good person, who would do her best for their people, as did most of the new representatives. But being in her new house with time to think was also, strangely sad and bittersweet, because while she loved living on Lyric again, on her family's old homestead, everything from her childhood was gone. And, she was so far from Cor.

They talked every night via vid screen and yet, she had no idea when or how they could be together again. Now that the elections were over, she had no real wish to live on the Jewel, at least not permanently. She fingered a little, silken bag she was carrying in her pocket to remind her of the decision she had to make.

Cor had been crowned Emperor soon after the Empress's death. It was still weird to think of him as Emperor. His first act had been to send in his forces and destroy the barbarian compound. He then confiscated and destroyed all the Gallaian drug fruit and candy equipment. The remaining Gallaians allowed Cor's inspectors in, claiming that Sying and her supporters had not had the approval of most Gallaians. The tenuous peace was holding. The trees he allowed them to keep, because of their remarkable radiation cleansing properties, but they were now highly regulated.

Meilin had returned to the Jewel to visit of course, for Emperor Cormorin's coronation and gala. And while their time together had been amazing, when they were able to steal some time alone, it wasn't enough. He'd been right when he'd said she was his match, but she wasn't sure how long they could make a long-distance relationship work. It was a two day journey between Lyric and Gallaius.

They were both busy, Cor with being Emperor, and Meilin, with seeing that her fledgling Office of Elections Integrity continued on into the future. There were so many ways for elections to go wrong. Meilin and the people she'd recruited were making sure that the playing field and results were fair and trustworthy. There would be no more Fongs in their future. Plus, in her spare time, she envisioned rebuilding her family's silk farm, and she was teaching local self-defense classes.

She and Cor disagreed sometimes, about what their future should hold, but they came up with the most delicious compromises. She found herself lost in a daydream when a Royal transport landed near the house. Had Cor sent her something again? He was always sending her sweet, sexy little surprises. She opened the door, expecting a delivery drone, but instead, Cor himself stepped out of the transport.

"Cor! What are you doing here?" She flew into his arms and he kissed her as if he hadn't seen her in a month, which, he hadn't. "I thought you weren't coming until next week."

"I couldn't wait that long. Congratulations! Lyric's first representative elections went off without a hitch. I knew you'd do it."

"Thank you." She grinned back. Some of the reps who won their districts weren't who she would have chosen, but the important thing was that they were who Lyrans had chosen.

Cor took a picnic basket out of the shuttle's refrigerator compartment. "I brought food," he teased, swinging the basket at her and leading the way across the yard and up a hill to where a single golden mulberry tree still stood. As soon as it put off seed, she'd be planting an orchard, and a few years down the road, bringing in silk worms.

He squinted up at the brilliant turquoise sky. "I can hardly get over the sky here," he said, putting the basket down under the tree. "And, I think I'd like to see more of it."

"Oh yeah?" She bit her lip and touched the little silk bag in her pocket.

"Yeah. I have a surprise for you." He took his com off his wrist and flicked it open, to an architectural hologram. She gasped and brought her hand to her throat, immediately choked up. It was an exact replica of her family's farmhouse and the silk barn nearby that she had accidentally burned as a teenager when her Gift had manifested after her parent's death. How had he found pictures? She sniffed.

"Lyric is so important to the Jewel, I figured it was about time we had a Royal home here, at least part of the time."

"Can you just, do that?" She looked up at him and blinked the moisture away.

"The Emperor can do that," he smiled with a twinge of uncertainty, "for his chosen Empress." He started to kneel down.

"Wait." She gave a little laugh and put her hand on his arm. She then took the silk bag out of her pocket and gulped, knowing her impulse to carry it had been right. She got down on one knee. "I thought maybe it was my turn."

She took two rings out of the little bag, one larger and one smaller. "They belonged to my grandparents." She took her grandfather's ring and held it up to him. It was a plain titanium band that still seemed to shine with love. "Emperor, will you—"

But he dropped to his knees with her and put his hands over hers. "Not Emperor, not between us. Just Cor."

She smiled and her eyes welled up again. "Cor, will you—"

"Yes." He cut her off with a kiss.

"Impatient," she mumbled.

"Mmhmm." But he let her put the ring on his finger. "Now let's see yours." And he slid her own titanium band onto her finger.

"They're not fancy," she said.

"No, they're perfect."

And it all began when an ex-soldier and her ex-prince exchanged rings beneath a mulberry tree....

WANT MORE FROM THE GALACTIC DREAMS UNIVERSE?

TAKE A SNEAK PEEK AT...

by

Bethany Maines

PART I:

Of Toads, Birds, & Dresses

One night, while she lay in her pretty bed, a large, ugly, wet toad crept through a broken pane of glass in the window, and leaped right upon the table where Thumbelina lay sleeping under her rose-leaf quilt. "What a pretty little wife this would make for my son," said the toad, and she took up the walnut-shell in which little Thumbelina lay asleep, and jumped through the window with it, into the garden.

Hans Christian Andersen, Thumbelina

Chapter 1:

THE AMBASSADOR ARRIVES AT THE TO'ANDAN BASE OF NEBULA SIX

Lina Tum-bel dangled by her ankles and considered her life. When she had accepted the position of ambassador to Earth's wayward former colonies, she had really thought there would be a lot more pomp and circumstance and a lot less brutality and mayhem. And a lot less toad people. Also, and not for nothing, a lot less toad-person crotch. If she was to be suspended by her feet, it seemed totally unnecessary that her face be at their groin level. It was like listening to a bunch of talking penises.

Penis number one was arguing for slitting her throat and cannibalizing her ship for parts. Penis number two was advocating for selling her and her crew to the nearest slave trader. And Penis number three was arguing for a combination of plans one and two, but with more rape and torture. There appeared to be some general resistance to the rape plan based on the fact that she and her crew were all so malformed and hideous. But also, why did Penis Three have to be *that* guy? She concurred that one should never be *that* guy, but thought *hideous* was a bit strong considering that their captors had protruding googly eyes, wide gaping mouths, bald heads, skin tinged to a greenish gray, and no necks to speak of—just shoulders melding seamlessly to ears.

After Earth's first interplanetary alliance had fallen to civil war, the planets and far bases, populated by enterprising human colonists, had been left on their own. Now, over seven hundred years after the first alliance failed, the people of Earth were once again reaching out to their former colonies, only to discover that their cousins no longer looked the same. Humans across the galaxy had used genetic manipulation to adapt to their far-flung homes. On a theoretical, diplomatic level, Lina found this acceptable, practical, and most likely necessary. On a personal level, she was finding the ick factor a bit stronger than expected.

Lina's mission was to visit the former children of Earth and bring them into the new interplanetary alliance. Aside from a few hiccups and misadventures, previous planets and bases had been mostly receptive. The bases in Nebula Six were proving to be deviations from the norm.

She twisted gently on her chain. As the mission leader, she'd been given a gold chain and ankle cuffs. She supposed that was a nice thought? She surveyed her fellow Terrans on their rusting steel chains. Poor Captain Aaro Carbanado was attempting to breathe through his own nose blood. First Mate Althea Fina looked as though she was about to pass out, and Petty Officer Edna McCoy was probably working on a cunning plan to blow something up. When it came to explosions, Edna could always be relied upon.

But was unconstrained detonation really the way to go in this situation?

Lina twisted again and surveyed the array of penises presented to her. They were all wearing some sort of codpiece. Only by cranking her neck up or down could she see more of their anatomy or clothing.

The guard next to her was wearing a full helmet and carapace that covered him from the shoulders up. The armor over his chest was well-defined, and the size of his codpiece was enough to make her wonder if genetic engineering had been deployed to affect other parts of their anatomy. The chain spun her the other way, and she decided that the guard was either naturally gifted or padding his codpiece.

She and the crew were dangling from an armature connected to a twenty-foot platform that hovered over the floor of a cavernous hanger deck. She had emerged from her ship—the *Tempest*, still moored a hundred feet above her head—and found herself stepping onto the floating platform to have what she had hoped would be a civil conversation with someone calling himself a prince. What had ensued was an ambush that resulted in the remaining crew locking themselves into the ship while she, the captain, the first mate, and the petty officer had found themselves unceremoniously clapped in chains and hauled up by their ankles. Thank goodness she'd worn pants.

The crew in the *Tempest* had not made any untoward moves as yet, but Lina knew that should matters turn serious, their standing orders were to blast their way out and return with an armada. Due to the vagaries of space travel, however, that process would likely take about three months. And, due the vagaries of her family, the portion of the fleet stationed nearest to their location was helmed by her older brother. Solving this matter here would be a lot more efficient and a lot less embarrassing at the next family gathering.

The argument above her was growing heated. The man-toad they were referring to as Prince, swayed by every new argument and his own waffling, was beginning to anger the others.

"Gentlemen," said Lina, deciding that there had been quite

enough nonsense, "while I appreciate all your plans and, clearly, some have more advantages than others"—there was a pause as they all tried to figure out which plans she thought were which, but she continued on, addressing the head penis—"I think the obvious solution is to send for the queen. She's really the one who ought to make the decisions, don't you think?" She had not yet ascertained whether the queen was the prince's mother or wife, but didn't take much reading of the room to have guessed that they were all scared of her.

"I think she's right," said the prince.

"Of course you think she's right," snapped another penis, who Lina thought was some sort of cousin to the prince. "You lay flat for anything with mammaries. You need to get with the modern times. Females aren't always right!"

"But usually," said the prince, "they are. Women are just more naturally able to make decisions. I know it's the latest fad to pre-tend men can have it all, and maybe that's fine for small things, but this is a matter of interbelt diplomacy."

"Interplanetary," corrected Lina. "I keep telling you, we're from Earth."

"Pull my egg sack and try another one," suggested the cousin. "You're all obviously Ránfuglar."

"But their ship doesn't look Ránfuglar," said the prince. "I think we should send for my mother."

"And that," boomed a commanding voice from the far end of the hangar deck, "is the smartest thing you've said today."

The penises parted and Lina was provided an upside-down view of a wide woman in a black dress who bullied her way across the floor, though not a single person stood in her way. Lina suspected that the queen was the type of person who would persecute air for being too breathable.

The monarch pushed her way to the forefront of the circle around Lina and her crew and stared at them, her left eye surveying the crew while her right stayed fixed on Lina.

"Good morning, Your Majesty," said Lina. "Allow me to introduce myself, I am Lina Tum-bel, ambassador of the Interplanetary Alliance."

The queen focused both eyes on Lina and bent over to inspect her more closely. She poked Lina with a long, slightly webbed finger. "Why are you hanging at this ridiculous height?"

"I had rather assumed it was a matter of advertisement," said Lina. The queen's eyes moved and left and right, taking in the view. Then she snorted.

"I've known them all since they were born. Trust me, there is not much to advertise." She stood up. "You"—she pointed at the guard closest to Lina—"put them at an appropriate level." The guard pushed a button on the controls, elevating Lina up to the queen's face level.

"Thanks," said Lina. She turned to the guard. "Thanks." He was startled into nodding. "Now, as I was attempting to say before we were attacked, we're from Earth, and we are on a mission of peace to reconnect with you, our long-lost cousins."

The queen snorted again. "We're not lost. You're the ones who went dark."

Lina had the feeling blunt speech was the queen's preferred way to communicate, so she tried a different tack. "Well, yes, but now that we've recovered from our few centuries of insanity, we thought we'd pop by and say hello."

"Just hello? Nothing along the lines of rebuilding the nutrient pipeline?"

"That idea has been floated in some circles," admitted Lina. The Nebula Six bases and nearby planets had previously supplied water and a vast array of minerals and elements, all of which were crucial to rebuilding the Alliance.

"I'm sure it has. We can talk about it, but the To'Anda will want competitive market incentives."

"I would be more than happy to discuss terms," said Lina. "But perhaps we could discuss them in a more upright position?"

"I suppose." The queen gestured to the guard again.

He let them all down with a rapid descent and hard drop at the end. It was difficult to come out of that looking dignified, but Lina attempted to rally.

"Right," she said, standing as quickly as possible and stepping forward. The rush of blood from her head left her light-headed, and she stumbled as she stepped down from the platform. A quick movement by the guard saved her from a face-plant, and she found herself clinging to his arm and staring at him with blurred vision. Had his eyeball just done something weird? More weird than the usual weird? Something digital? Lina realized she was staring and pulled herself together.

Once right side up, she realized that, while the men were more or less the usual height, she was significantly shorter than the To'Andan woman. She could tell the queen was used to in-timidating others with her size, but Lina's family all used the same trick, and if it didn't work over who got to shower first, it wasn't going to work here.

"Well," said Lina, smiling, "hello, so nice to see you from this angle."

"Why didn't you just rotate your eyes?" asked the prince, inspecting her from a distance she considered rather too close.

"Ah," said Lina, not backing up. "Interesting thought. But I'm afraid our eyes don't do that."

"Deficient," said the queen.

"Most likely," agreed Lina. "But we do make up for it by being able to turn our heads." She demonstrated neck movement.

"That makes your spinal column too easy to damage," said the cousin. "Also, it's weird-looking."

The queen reached out and slapped the back of his head. "Don't be rude to our guest. It's not her fault she's unfortunate-looking. Now then, Ambassador, if you would care to accompany me, we can discuss matters."

"My crew?" asked Lina.

"Will stay here," said the queen. She gestured to the guard, who nudged Lina forward. Lina glanced back at her crew. At least she'd gotten them right side up. Now all she had to do was get them out of this alive.

ABOUT THE AUTHOR

Karen Harris Tully creates elaborate worlds for her novels aided by her bachelor's in political science and economics. After growing up in the snowy mountains of Colorado, Karen experienced the traffic nightmare of Seattle before accidentally realizing she's a small-town girl. She happily lives in Raymond, WA, singing karaoke with her amazingly supportive husband, two beautiful children, and one hyper feline.

I love hearing from readers. Connect with me for more information on my upcoming books:

» *karenharristully.com*
» *facebook.com/ KarenHarrisTully*
» *karenharristully.tumblr.com*
» *twitter: @KHarrisTully*

OTHER WORKS BY KAREN HARRIS TULLY

Karen Harris Tully is the
author of The Faarian Chronicles:
EXILE, a 2017 Kindle Book Awards Finalist.

THE FAARIAN CHRONICLES

Exile

Inheritance

Extinction

GALACTIC DREAMS

2019